The Doberman howled in anguish. Summoning all his strength, he struggled to his feet, weaving his head to escape the swiping paws of the insistent tabby. He kicked his hind legs furiously at the Blue which was mauling his stomach, and violently jerked his whole body to displace the assailant from his back. In a desperate lunge he twisted and caught the Blue in his jaws, tearing it roughly away from his bleeding testicles. His teeth bit straight through the shrieking animal.

As Wolf turned, the tabby leapt straight at his exposed neck and took a firm hold. The Doberman, a new surge of pain acting as a spur to his efforts, rolled over quickly onto his back, crushing the short-hair instantly and stunning the tabby. He spat out the Blue which he still held between his clenched fangs and rolled swiftly back onto his legs.

The tabby, now recovered, and lying on the dog's blind side, rushed once more for Wolf's throat, its small, jagged teeth gaining a deadly grip on the main artery. Blood spurted from under the dog's chin. Wolf threshed his head up and down until he had shaken the cat free, and then started to crawl back towards the house, each painful step accompanied by a rattling sound from his torn throat...

Wolf slumped on the top step, extended his paw to the door and scraped at the white paintwork in a last, pathetic attempt to gain entrance before his head rolled despairingly over and the stiffness left his sleek body.

He lay once more as if asleep, loose and relaxed, as he had been minutes earlier—before the arrival of the cats.

CW00683895

THE CATS

BY NICK SHARMAN

To my beloved wife Sara,
for making me so very happy

and to my splendid son Alex,
for making me so very proud

CHAPTER ONE

The young boy moved purposefully between the two parallel lines of mesh cages that filled the narrow white room. His brow was furrowed in concentration and his tongue poked out of the right-hand corner of his mouth.

At each cage he bent down, removed a white plastic container that was attached to the side, filled it with two pieces of dried fish, slid it back into position and moved on.

The room was becoming increasingly silent, the uneven clicks of his metal shoe-heels accompanied only by the soft hum of air-conditioning and the pathetic mewings of animals waiting to receive their meal.

When he had filled and replaced the last container he turned, leant against the door leading to the outside of the flat and looked around the room. In the distance he could hear the squeal of brakes and tires as lorries slowed down in their approach to the nearby motorway. The noises were faint and detached, half-heard as if in a dream.

The boy glanced at his watch and saw that it was almost time to return to school. But he still hadn't finished. He had to give out the milk and wash out the food containers. He mentally ticked off the list of his duties and, satisfied that he had done everything else asked of him, began to walk back up the corridor towards the main part of the L-shaped laboratory.

As he moved, he could feel their eyes on him. The animals had finished eating and were waiting, watching him. Nervously he swept back a lock of hair, stared straight ahead and fixed his gaze on the wooden racks of test tubes and labeled bottles on the far wall. But soon his eyes began to flicker from side to side, nervously searching the dark interior of each cage as he passed. Occasionally, he could just make out the gleam of an unfriendly and accusing eye. For the first time since entering the room he began to doubt the wisdom of accepting the American's offer. He had agreed because he liked being near animals; he felt an affinity for them, and it was a way to escape the cold loneliness of school lunch hours. But now he sensed sinister vibrations coming from the cages and wondered if the pain and the bullying might not have been preferable.

His heart began to thump and the palms of his hands were sticky with sweat despite the artificial coolness of the room. If he could just get to the end of the line. Why was it taking so long? He suppressed an urge to run. What would be the use? He would have to retrace his steps back down the corridor in order to get out onto the street, and he still had to feed the animals their milk and clean their containers.

He tried to think of more pleasant things, but his concentration was disturbed by the wave of nausea that seemed to start in his stomach and roll up through his body and into his throat. He choked back the acidic liquid. What a time for his kidneys to start acting up. The disease which had made him a "delicate" child, giving his skin an unhealthy pallor and discoloring his teeth, reacted on him at the first sign of stress. He took deep breaths, gulping down air, and ploughed on. If he collapsed, he would certainly die, for he needed dialysis immediately and the American was not expected back for several days.

The acrid taste persisted. Quite unconsciously he removed a piece of fish from one of the bowls and nibbled at it. The taste was so foul he spat it out, and spat vigorously several times before carrying on. *What a stupid thing to do,* he thought. Only water would clear the taste. He took another step forward. Only five yards to go.

The strip lights began to flicker and then went out. The gentle breath of the air-conditioner was like a death rattle as it fell away.

The boy stood rooted to the spot. The silence was devastating. In the dim light which filtered through the dirty windows of the basement flat, he could barely make out the end of the corridor.

The nameless terrors of darkness crowded in on the boy and he started running, smashing into something and knocking it to the ground. He cursed and pressed on, limping badly. When he had reached the desk at the end of the row of cages nearest the window, he turned and peered into the darkness to assess the damage. He could vaguely see one of the cages lying at an angle across the corridor, and wondered whether the cat was all right.

Turning back to the desk, he began rummaging through the drawers and sighed with relief as he found the familiar cold metal cylinder.

He switched the torch on … and screamed. In the brilliant light, frozen in mid-leap, something was flying towards him, sharp white teeth and outstretched talons heading for his face. He fell backwards, still yelling, the torch fell from his hand and broke on the stone floor.

Quickly, he struggled to his feet, automatically brushing imagined dust from his corduroy trousers. It could only have been the cat from the overturned cage. He was thankful that he had seen it first. God knows what his reaction might have been had it hit him in the darkness. Still, the shock had been bad enough. He leant against the desk while his body juddered with the furious pumping action of his heart.

He was soaked in sweat and the room was getting hotter by the second. The electricity had gone out for some reason which meant that the air-conditioner would not work either. The room was catching up with the temperature outside, and this was the worst day so far of the hottest summer London had ever known. It was well over a hundred degrees Fahrenheit.

At length his heartbeat decreased, but, by now, his hair was sticking to his scalp and the sweat was beginning to trickle down from his armpits. He took off his jacket, loosened his tie and began unbuttoning his shirt. All thoughts of escape disappeared as his body began to bum with the heat. He felt himself beginning to choke. The nausea had returned and he buckled over, vomiting putrid liquid onto the ground. The smell mingled with the sickening stench of the cats.

Painfully he raised himself to a standing position. His leg

still hurt, but his attention was diverted from his physical misery by the sound of paws pattering up the corridor. Whether they were moving towards or away from him, he couldn't tell. Then he noticed that the other cats had begun to pace up and down in their cages, obviously excited by the cat on the ground.

The boy listened, fascinated as a loud clang sounded in the room and was followed by another and another. The cats were hurling themselves against the steel mesh of the cage doors, trying to escape. Slowly the violent noises ebbed away to be replaced by a more terrifying sound, the high-pitched screech of grinding metal. They were trying to chew their way out through the wire, gnawing with growing frenzy as the heat increased. Within seconds the shrieking had become a crazy din.

The boy felt increasingly faint as he continued undressing. He shrugged off his shoes, and, undoing his belt, slid his trousers down to his ankles and stepped out of them. He stood, swaying slightly, and looking down, saw the freed cat staring up at him.

He could feel his mind going. *None of this is fair,* he thought. The cat continued to stare. Something had to be done for them. He shook his head. Only one thought stood out from the confused jumble in his mind. *Free the cats.* They had to be free.

As if in a trance he moved to the first cage and tentatively twisted the screw on the small metal bar which held the door in position. The cat inside stopped trying to escape and crept backwards. The boy tugged at the bar and it began to give way. He hesitated at the last moment. From the back of the cage the crouching cat mewed. The boy yanked at the bar and the door swung free, clanking as it lazily reached the end of its arc.

The cat leapt to the ground and the boy moved to the next cage and opened it, more quickly this time and without any hesitation. Soon he was running from one to the next, his bare feet padding on the floor. When he reached the end of the line, he leant once more against the door, an inexplicable excitement mounting within him. His hand slipped to the latch, and grinning wildly, he launched himself forward and raced down the corridor, scattering the cats before him. Halfway down he tripped on the fallen cage, crashed forward, face to the floor and lay for a moment, his mind a mass of previously unfelt thoughts and emotions.

He felt clean, natural, free and there was a sense of affinity, of belonging; something he had never felt before. The cats crowded around him and ran over his body, paws slipping in his sweat, fur brushing by turns roughly and caressingly over his skin, teeth nipping gently, exquisitely at his exposed flesh, mouths nuzzling against his face. He turned onto his back and began to laugh joyously, louder and louder, his legs threshing ecstatically as he grabbed at the sea of fur in which he swam, his spine arching further and further from the ground.

He felt a huge, throbbing, thrusting power flowing through him. His stomach arched outwards once more until his head almost touched the skin on his back. His body tautened until it seemed the muscles would burst, and then he screamed a scream of release and fainted, his twisted limbs straightening until he lay flat against the floor.

CHAPTER TWO

Envious eyes stared at the small Italian sports car as it purred through the terraced slums of North London. Within twenty minutes it was speeding past the industrial workers' houses that spread along the sides of the A10 route to Cambridge. When the buildings on either side of the road had been replaced by endless, dull, flat fields, the driver wound down both windows and nestled back in his seat. He breathed deeply. The air was pure and tasted good.

John Inglis had grown up in West Virginia, where people were used to the boiling sun and stifling humidity. They expected it and fitted their lives around it. But the people of London never expected it and the city just hadn't been built to cope with it. There was only one place to be in England when it got this hot—in a fast car on a country road. Inglis smiled. This felt almost as good as sex. As he drove he reached into the cramped back seat of the car and grasped a can of lager from a large crate. He ripped the tab off with his teeth, choked off the liquid in three long pulls, crumpled the can in one fist, and threw it over his shoulder. He exhaled loudly and burped. He felt deeply contented—so contented that he didn't notice the Spaniel until far too late. It was staring balefully at him from twenty yards away, smack in the middle of his path.

He swerved the car wildly, praying that he had missed the animal, slammed hard on the brakes and came to a shuddering halt. Perhaps his father had been right. Perhaps he should never have taken up driving. His concentration wandered far too easily. Another driver would have seen the damn dog from miles away and he had missed it by inches. If the road had been wet he would probably have ended up a dead man, and he wasn't ready to die quite yet.

He reached out to his glove compartment, pulled out a crumpled packet of American non-tipped cigarettes, lit one and inhaled deeply. His hands were shaking as he opened the car door and hoisted himself out into the hot daylight.

He looked around for the dog, but there was no sign of it. The only life for miles was a black saloon car, oddly old-fashioned with bulbous wings, parked some fifty yards behind him on the road. Odd, he thought, it hadn't been there before. Suddenly he was aware that it had been tailing him. He had seen it every time he looked in his rear-view mirror but had failed to note the fact consciously.

Inglis began to walk towards the car but stopped after a few steps. It was strangely threatening. The whole scene reminded him of something in a Hitchcock film. The hero is standing at a crossroads. It is a scorching summer day. The surrounding countryside is flat and deserted. There is a plane in the distance spraying crops. It circles closer and closer. Nothing else is moving in that sinister landscape. Only at the last moment, as the plane swoops down, does the hero realize that he is the target. The plane is trying to kill him and there is nowhere to hide.

Inglis felt just like that, totally exposed, stranded halfway between his own car and the stranger's. He peered into the windshield to catch a glimpse of the driver, but the sun reflected fiercely off the glass.

Without warning the saloon clunked into gear and Inglis had to stop himself from crying out in fright. To his intense relief it rolled backwards, bumping oddly. When it stopped, Inglis could see what had made its movement awkward. In front of the ponderous, menacing bonnet lay the squashed remains of the Spaniel, its soft. appealing eyes bulging lifelessly from their sockets.

A flood of anger swept away his fear. True, he experimented on animals in a laboratory, but this was different. The death was unnecessary. The driver could have avoided the dog, but had chosen instead to kill it in cold blood.

Inglis wiped the sweat from his thick moustache, bringing

his thumb and index finger round in an arc on either side of his mouth, made a swift, obscene gesture at the unseen driver and ran back to his own car.

He knew why the car was following him. All on account of an obsessive old man who refused to let go.

"OK, baby," Inglis purred at the machine as he gunned it into life, "I read all about your fantastic acceleration. Now let's see you in action."

The wheels shredded the roadside gravel, sending it shooting upwards in fierce jets, and then the car was hurtling forward. He felt the engine shake as he pushed it to the limit in each gear. By the time he jettisoned into fourth the needle was wavering past a hundred on the speedometer. "Go, honey," he screamed in exhilaration.

The telegraph poles by the roadside looked like a picket fence. He glanced in his mirror. Almost unbelievably, the saloon had kept up with him and now seemed to be gaining.

"Son of a bitch," Inglis muttered between clenched teeth. "You're going to pay for this."

Inglis knew just what to do to fulfill the promise. Twenty breathless minutes later they were approaching Blaxborough. He decided to gamble on the chance that his pursuer was unfamiliar with the road. The road began to steepen imperceptibly into a small hill. The accident warning signs by the side of the road were a vague blur. There was no way that the driver behind could make them out. Inglis geared down hurriedly and hit the crest at a manageable fifty in time to swerve out of the way of the ditch that separated the oncoming driver from an open field. Once Inglis had negotiated the ninety-degree turn in the road, he brought the car to a halt and waited.

The black saloon came over the crest doing over eighty miles an hour, veered madly, leapt the ditch, hit the furrowed field and somersaulted spectacularly, ending up on its back, rocking gently to and fro.

Inglis laughed as he pulled away.

"Welcome to Blaxborough," he chortled. His damned father. That sick old man had been hunting him for over a year. So, he wanted his son back in the States by his side. Well, Inglis was

going to do his best to deny him that pleasure. For on
moment he found himself hoping that the goon in the b.
was dead.

"Thought we'd seen the last of you, sir."

Inglis gave the porter a wry look as he passed by the Porter's
Lodge and entered Trinity Great Court, his heart still pumping
from the car chase.

He walked briskly down the gravel path in that peculiarly
loose-limbed American way, drinking in once again the splen-
dors of that expansive rectangle with its smooth lawns, ornate
fountain and cobbled pavements. He passed the dining hall
and slipped through to the medieval peace of Neville's Court.
He went straight to the first door in the cloisters, stopped for
a moment, smiled at the familiar arched Gothic doorway and
knocked quietly.

The door was immediately flung open to reveal an aged
Cambridge academic dressed in tweed sports jacket, flannel
trousers and scuffed suede shoes. The old gentleman, a mass
of elongated arms and legs, goggled at his visitor for a second.

"Good God," he exclaimed, removing his pipe. "John, dear
boy, how absolutely bloody wonderful to see you." He grabbed
hold of Inglis's arm and dragged him into the musty room. "Sit
down by the fire there. Not lit, of course. Too damned hot. Take
a drink, won't you? No, I remember, Scotch. I still haven't got
around to buying any bourbon. Filthy drink anyway. Well, this
is a surprise."

Inglis laughed good-naturedly and accepted the huge
tumbler that had been thrust affectionately into his hands. He
glanced around the room and sniffed with fond nostalgia at the
familiar aroma of antique books and caramel pipe-tobacco that
had been so much a part of his own college days in that academy.

Bertram Vole, Professor of Microbiology, plumped into his
favorite armchair, splashing whisky over his jacket.

"Go on, drink up. Don't sip! You don't mind it neat, do you?
It's the best malt in the college—I've polished off the rest. I'm
back working with the government. Nothing nasty but it's still
top secret and I can't tell you about it."

Inglis looked at him questioningly.

"Well," continued the professor, "perhaps I'll tell you just a bit about it later on if you promise not to peach on me. Official Secrets Act and all that."

Inglis smiled. The old man had never been very safe with secrets.

"You've given me quite a shock. First a series of letters with no address at the top, each with a Paddington postmark on the envelope." The old man's eye for detail had not left him. "And then silence for six months. Probably living under an assumed name to get away from dear old Daddy, I shouldn't wonder."

Inglis choked on his drink. The professor ignored him and carried on.

"Well, never mind about that. Tell me what you've been up to. I'm pleased to hear that you're still involved in scientific experiment, but I'm afraid that you're not making great advances in bacteriology with that last piece of research you wrote to me about. I've been over all that ground myself. I could have written to you and placed you firmly on the right path if only you'd left an address. Well, what is the boy genius engaged upon?"

Inglis placed his glass on the table by his elbow and fished in his pocket for a cigarette before starting.

"You're right, as usual. I have been living under an assumed name. Sources back in the States informed me my father was looking for me again and I just want to forget about the bastard. Apparently he's had detectives out scouring the countryside."

"Couldn't he have found out from the American Embassy or the police?"

"He's too frightened of the publicity. Anyway, the authorities wouldn't have a hope of finding me. There are thousands of people in this country who don't have the right to be here. My visa ran out months ago."

The professor nodded. "Your father has been looking for you. One of his detectives came here recently. Said he was from the Embassy. Of course I didn't believe a word of it. I threw him out and phoned the Embassy. They'd never heard of the blighter."

Inglis grinned. "Well, they've found me now. One of them followed me up here."

The professor was startled. "Where is he now?"

"In hospital. I sort of made him crash."

"Well done," the professor enthused. "Your father must be a very determined old bird to want you back when you so obviously despise him."

"They're going to run him for president next year, I read in the papers. He wants me back by his side during the campaign. That way he can appeal to the family voters and keep his eye on me at the same time. There's enough skeletons in his past to occupy the press without them having a renegade son to write about. After I fed the newspapers that story about my sister—it was true by the way, every word of it—I'm surprised he didn't take out a contract on my life. That would really suit his style. Perhaps he has already, who knows? I wouldn't put anything past him."

"Tell me," the professor gazed earnestly at his old pupil, "is that why you hate him so much, because of what happened to your sister?"

A look of pain flashed across Inglis's face and an image formed in his mind. A plain, dumpy girl, her face puffed and blue, her swollen tongue poking obscenely from her puffed lips as her ungainly body swung slowly, back and forth, from the end of a rope attached to an attic rafter. Inglis blinked his eyes savagely several times. The image came to him again and again in dreams. He didn't want to face it during his waking hours as well. Telling the papers had been a form of catharsis.

"Professor, it's a long story. I appreciate your concern, but I don't really want to talk about it. I've got something far more important to discuss."

The old man got up and walked back to the drinks table. "I understand, John. Please carry on."

Inglis cleared his throat and began. "During the first term of my last year I attended a special course you were giving. It was outside the exam curriculum and only a handful of undergraduates attended. It was, I'm sure you'll remember, 'Biological Warfare—the Science and the Morality'."

"I remember it well," the professor chuckled. "I almost got booted out of the Department as a result, professor or no professor. A bit revolutionary for the Science Faculty, although you left-wing youngsters lapped it up. What about it?"

"It was a course of eight lectures. The first four dealt with the classic diseases used in such warfare. You gave us a few hints about modern research and the direction it was leading and the next three lectures dealt with the morality of the whole thing. I seem to remember that you defended it fairly well despite a couple of people storming out in disgust. At the end of the seventh lecture you promised to make the last one really interesting. You were going to talk about animals and refused to give any further hints. Well, I waited with a good deal of excitement for the next week, but when the time came, the lecture had been cancelled. We were told that you were suffering from 'overwork' and had gone on a sabbatical for two terms."

The professor had stopped making his drinks during Inglis's monologue. A nervous tick had begun to flicker below his left eye.

"I knew that wasn't true. You were in the best of spirits all term. Someone had put the clamp on you and I had the feeling it was something to do with the proposed lecture."

The old man turned from the drinks table and walked slowly, empty-handed, back to his chair.

"Although you didn't say anything further about the animals, you left us some pretty cryptic mimeographed notes on the course, as you always did. Each page referred to the substance of each lecture. Your notes on the final lecture contained a few diagrams, a couple of hints, some points for discussion, test analyses, and a funny little drawing of an animal in the bottom left-hand corner. You always had a little joke in there somewhere."

The blood had drained from the professor's face. Inglis, slightly perturbed at the effects his words were having, nevertheless carried on.

"When I had finished my last piece of research—you were right, it was all nonsense—I looked around for something else to do. I had to make a name for myself somehow. Getting sent down for political agitation isn't the greatest boost to a scientist's career. So I remembered your lecture and I dug out the notes and, knowing what I did about your methods, began to piece the experiments together."

"What stage have you reached?" The professor's voice was a faint whisper.

"Way beyond where you stopped. I'm on the verge of something big. Very big and I'm sure you've got the key to the final stage. In fact, I'm pretty suspicious that you've reached that point ahead of me."

"Which animals did you use for the experiments?"

"Cats, just as you suggested. That was the picture, wasn't it. You aren't a very good artist."

The old man's eyes narrowed. The only sound in the room for a moment was his hoarse breathing.

"I only have one question to ask you."

Inglis leant forward in anticipation.

"Have you subjected the animals to intense heat?"

CHAPTER THREE

In front of a dignified white Edwardian mansion standing some twenty yards from West London's busy Bayswater Road, hidden from prying eyes by an elegant line of beech trees, lay Wolf. Around the large dog's neck was a studded metal collar attached to a ten-foot leash. His sweating tongue lolled languidly, and a small puddle of liquid had collected on the ground next to his mouth.

The animal looked peaceful, but that was only a camouflage masking the natural instincts of breed. In Thuringia, Germany, in the 1880s Herr Louis Dobermann, a tax-collector, had hit on a scheme to render his door-to-door visits safer. Using a mixture of the Rottweiler, the old German Pinscher and the tenacious Manchester Terrier, he bred a dog of supreme loyalty, intelligence, watchfulness and strength, with one feature more important than any other—a savagery formerly unknown amongst domestic breeds. Wolf had all the qualities; he would attack without question and kill without a flicker of concern.

He had been imported from Germany as a puppy by an English security firm. After two years of intense and rigorous training, he had become easily the finest dog on their lists. When the company had been asked to provide an animal for their most prestigious job, protecting a British Cabinet Minister, they had had no hesitation in sending Wolf.

Fred Dempsey, former Minister of State for Northern Ireland, had decided on nothing but the best when it came to protecting his property and his life. His term of office had been brief—his policy of appeasement and negotiation with the terrorists had made him unpopular with all sides, including the terrorists, who regarded him as weak. But in that short time he had managed to earn himself a place on the IRA death list. Right at the very top. The police had offered their help but Dempsey had remained skeptical of their abilities. Too many prominent Ulster businessmen had been assassinated for anyone to feel safe with official protection. When his move to the more sedate pastures of the Ministry of Education had failed to halt the threatening letters, sinister phone calls and clumsily disguised letter-bombs, Dempsey had called in a private security firm.

Immediately, his house had been transformed into a fortress whose moat consisted of a series of sophisticated electronic alarms set to be triggered by the slightest unexplained movement. To this excellent defense system had been added Tom, Wolf's handler, armed with an arsenal of anti-personnel devices and specially trained in letter-bomb disposal. He was permanently stationed inside the house where he kept a constant watch on the defense gadgetry, checked the post and answered all telephone calls.

The grounds of the house were Wolf's domain. During the day he was there for show. Burglars or would-be assassins would have to think twice before attempting to get past such a beast. But it was at night when he came into his own, when his trained vision and heightened sense of smell made him as perceptive as any piece of technology … and far more lethal.

While Fred Dempsey slept as well as any politician's conscience would allow him, Wolf slunk silently through the shadows, a sleek, black shadow himself, ears pricked, senses twitching—a superb machine. Herr Louis Dobermann would have been proud of him.

Wolf raised his head slightly, yawned and subsided back into a state of semi-sleep.

Inside the house, all was silent. The three domestic servants had made use of their master's attendance at the House of Commons to go picnicking in Kensington Gardens. Tom, exhausted by the crisis of a temporary power cut earlier in the day, had gone downstairs to cool himself with a damp cloth. The basement kitchen had been soothingly cool and he had decided to sit for a moment in the cook's chair. Within seconds he had been fast asleep, his chest rising and falling gently.

He was still asleep when Wolf's black nose twitched. The dog's eyes flicked open and glinted in the sun. He could smell an old enemy. He started up, nostrils contracting violently, his flanks shifting minutely as he sought the source of the odor.

From the foliage at the bottom of the garden, came two pinpoints of reflected light. The cat, a lithe tabby, sauntered from the trees and came to rest some fifteen yards from the dog in the middle of the lawn. It was still for an instant and then its hackles rose and its legs straightened. Its spine arched upwards and it spat. Then, just as quickly, it was silent again, resuming its relaxed standing position. Its eyes were expressionless slits.

Wolf padded forward to the end of his leash, loping down the stairs, displaying no emotion as he moved smoothly forward, as brutally cold as a professional killer. The leather leash tautened. He stopped, stood for a moment, sizing up the situation, and lay down flat on his stomach with his paws pointing straight ahead, hind legs tensed, his body compact, coiled, waiting.

The cat came forward a few more yards until he was almost within striking distance of the dog. Their eyes locked, and, much to Wolf's surprise, the cat showed no fear. With every other animal he had ever met he had smelt the panic at once, the energizing, tingling stench of terror. But now he could smell no fear at all. If anything, it was quite the opposite, with the cat exuding such a steady, quiet aggression that Wolf's eyes flickered away from its pointed gaze.

That seemed to act as a signal, as, with bewildering speed, other shadows flitted from the undergrowth. The dog, belly to the ground, was beginning to experience a new emotion and he edged backwards, hind legs working frantically. He was tasting fear for the first time in his life and he had no liking for it.

The tabby, when Wolf had steeled himself sufficiently to look at it once more, had been joined by three companions. A new shock of fear waved through him as he tried to keep them all in view at once, desperately alert to any sudden movement. To the far right of the tabby was a Siamese, a Lilac-Point with pinkish fur, bat-like ears and piercing blue eyes. On either side of it stood a Russian Blue and a black and white short-hair.

None of them stirred, but as Wolf's hind legs began to scramble backwards up the stairs in an ungainly fashion, the four cats eased forward. By the time the dog had reached the door, they were at the base of the stairs. Wolf began to whine softly for his handler. It was a sound comprised of shame and fear.

As he gazed at his enemies, he noticed with an extra thrill of terror that their eyes were no longer devoid of expression and, looking deep into the almond-shaped openings, he could discern a terrible, mindless hunger growing there.

The huge black dog was hypnotized, transfixed. Its muscles stiffened, its eyes glazed over. Short, sharp bleating sounds of supplication rose from its throat.

The Siamese hissed suddenly and its swishing front paw described an arc through the air.

The spell was broken.

Wolf snapped to attention, his fear gone, back in command of himself. There was no hesitation. He pounced forward with startling speed, engulfing the Siamese in a snap of his powerful jaws. The cat screeched as the dog's enormously long, razor-sharp teeth pierced its fur and crushed its internal organs. Wolf tossed the carcass aside nonchalantly and turned to face his remaining would-be assailants.

The other cats had retreated to their original position and sat staring first at their dead companion and then into the eyes of the murderous Doberman.

The dog emitted a blood-curdling growl from the depths of its throat and bared its gleaming, blood-drenched fangs. Its muscles tensed. It sprang, jaws gaping, straight for the tabby. The cat moved swiftly backwards and the growl stopped dead in Wolf's throat as his head snapped back in mid-flight. The leather leash had brought him up inches short of his target.

He lay for a moment on the ground, panting, half choked, trying to regain the breath he had lost on impact. The cats were on him at once. The tabby swiped at the fallen giant's eyes, its talons digging parallel grooves in the soft membrane of the pupil. The Russian Blue flew straight for the exposed underbelly, teeth sinking savagely into the scrotal sack. The short-hair

leapt onto the Doberman's back, scratching and tearing fero-
ciously at the sleek fur.

Wolf howled in anguish. Summoning all his strength he
struggled to his feet, weaving his head to escape the swiping
paws of the insistent tabby. He kicked his hind legs furiously
at the Blue which was mauling at his stomach, and violently
jerked his whole body to displace the assailant from his back.
In a desperate lunge he twisted and caught the Blue in his jaws,
tearing it roughly away from his bleeding testicles. His teeth bit
straight through the shrieking animal.

As Wolf turned, the tabby leapt straight at his exposed neck
and took a firm hold. The Doberman, a new surge of pain acting as a spur to his efforts, rolled over quickly onto his back,
crushing the short-hair instantly and stunning the tabby. He
spat out the Blue which he still held between his clenched fangs
and rolled swiftly back onto his legs.

The tabby, now recovered, and lying on the dog's blind side,
rushed once more for Wolf's throat, its small, jagged teeth gaining a deadly grip on the main artery. Blood spurted from under
the dog's chin. Wolf threshed his head up and down until he
had shaken the cat free, and then started to crawl back towards
the house, each painful step accompanied by a rattling sound
from his torn throat.

As the dog heaved himself up the half-dozen steps leading
to the door, the tabby darted frenetically back and forth across
the lawn, hauling the bodies of its dead companions back to the
undergrowth at the end of the front lawn. By the time that Wolf
had reached the door, the lawn was clear of bodies. The only
evidence of the battle was the blood glistening evilly in the pale
sunlight like red oil.

Wolf slumped on the top step, extended his paw to the door
and scraped at the white paintwork in a last, pathetic attempt to
gain entrance before his head rolled despairingly over and the
stiffness left his sleek body.

He lay once more as if asleep, loose and relaxed, as he had
been minutes earlier—before the arrival of the cats.

CHAPTER FOUR

"No, I haven't subjected them to unusual heat."

The professor was obviously relieved. "In that case, we should be all right." The color began steadily to return to his cheeks.

"Professor, why is the temperature so important?"

"It's the key to the whole thing."

"In what way?"

"The extraordinary facet of the bacteria which you isolated is that it only becomes fully active inside the body. You will, no doubt, have noticed a certain restlessness in the animals; sudden movements, continual pacing of the cage, and other similar symptoms."

Inglis nodded.

"That is the normal reaction at room temperature. Once it had reached beyond one hundred and five degrees Fahrenheit, the picture changes in a horrifying way. The very nature of the bacteria changes."

"In what way?" Inglis's voice was breathless with anticipation.

"I'd rather not tell you," the professor replied, coyly. "It was foolish of me to provide you with those lecture notes when I hadn't taken the experiments to their conclusion. I was convinced that I was on the trail of something pretty damned important. It had struck me as odd that biological warfare had always been targeted at humans. I began to wonder what would happen if a sufficiently powerful virus could be created with the sole aim of affecting specific animal species. The resulting chaos might prove immense and the target country would have few grounds to suspect foul play. So I set about creating that bacteria. I thought I was on to something, but I didn't know quite how big it was until the week before that last lecture was due to be delivered. The results of my final experiment here in Cambridge were so ghastly that there was no choice but to involve the government. After I'd recovered from the experience, the Ministry of Defence signed me up to carry on my research under its auspices."

Inglis shook his head sadly.

"Now don't be sanctimonious with me, young man. Being asked to work for your country is a great honor for a scientist, especially when they beg you and place almost limitless funds at your disposal. That is why you were told that I had taken a sabbatical. I ended up working at Porton Down for almost nine months. Oh, I know I had paid lip-service to morality and science up till then, but the project was just too exciting, too important to turn down. The scientist got the better part of me for a while, but then I began to see the terrifying implications of what I had started, and I resigned."

"But you're back working with the government."

"Certainly, but there's nothing nasty about it this time. All quite innocent. I assure you."

Inglis looked skeptical.

The professor spoke sharply. "Rather than sitting there looking pious, I suggest you phone your flat and make sure that everything is all right."

"Now, Professor, what could go wrong? Besides, the kid'll be back at school by now."

"Now look, John, I'm being deadly serious. I've seen what happens when this experiment's a success. It's too frightening to contemplate. Just check for my sake. If nothing has happened, I'll motor down with you and arrange for the animals and your samples to be handed over to the authorities. I'll make sure that nothing happens to you, don't worry."

Inglis rose from his seat with a resigned expression, walked over to the telephone sitting on the professor's desk and dialed the number of an old German lady that lived in his block of flats. As he waited for her to answer the phone, thoughts raced through his mind. He wondered what on earth could have had such a deep effect on the normally unflappable Professor.

"Hello, Mrs. Geist. Ah, good. You recognize my voice. No, I'm not phoning from my room. No, I'm somewhere else right now. That's right." He sighed and stared at the ceiling. "Look, Mrs. Geist, could you please go down to my flat and make sure that everything is all right? Well, just listen for anything unusual, any strange noises. No, it's nothing to be afraid of, I assure you." He listened for a moment with a pained expression on his face as a gabble of broken English flooded down the phone. Suddenly his knuckles gripped hard round the telephone. "You had a what?" His hands began to shake. "How hot?" he said quietly. "Please go down at once, Mrs. Geist, but, whatever you do, don't go into the room."

The professor started to speak, but Inglis motioned for him to be quiet. The babble started up once more. Inglis listened for a few seconds. The phone slipped from his fingers, thudding dully on the floor, the old German lady's voice coming through like a crazed mynah bird.

He turned slowly to the professor.

"How bad were the results of your experiments?"

The old man's face told him the answer.

The ball of spit splashed messily against Mark Dempsey's cheek. He brushed quickly past the group of laughing louts lounging around the entrance to the classroom and walked to his desk at the back of the large, echoing room. He weaved unsteadily as he moved.

He had not felt right since lunch, not since the moment he had awakened, naked and frightened, on the cold stone floor of the American's laboratory. The strip lighting had pained his eyes and the sound of the air-conditioner had seemed like a roar in his ears. In a daze he had got onto his feet and had spent several minutes stumbling around the room retrieving his discarded clothing. It had only been when pulling on his trousers that he had noticed the absence of the cats and the door gaping open at the end of the corridor.

He had stood, gazing around himself in panic, wracking

his mind for some memory of the events of the previous hour. Images had begun to whirl in snatches before him: walking down the corridor; fear; the lights going out; bumping into a cage; searching for a torch; something soft brushing against him; a sense of intense exhilaration; his body tingling with pleasure. He had had no problem recalling small events, but had been unable to piece them together in any cohesive fashion.

Walking back to school, stooping occasionally to rub at a painful bruise on his leg, he had thought of the American and what he would say on his return. The man had explained to him, in his lazy Southern states drawl, how nearly a year's work had gone into the cats and how important it was that nothing untoward befell them. He would just have to tell him the truth. After all, there was nothing much, Mark reflected, that he could do about it now, and as to whether he was guilty of anything he could not tell without remembering the incidents more clearly.

By the time he reached school, the first lesson had begun and he sneaked off to the toilets for a rest. It was the only part of the building where the young boy could escape his tormentors. He sat for half an hour in one of the cubicles thinking, with an aching nostalgia, about his old school. Bruton Academy had been a perfect, smug, self-satisfied little world for a shy, bespectacled bookworm like Mark. He had been truly happy there for four years and had been poised to enter into the school's senior section in the following year. His father had already bought him the blue uniform with gold braid that he would be clad in for five years while working towards university.

And then the bomb had dropped.

Fred Dempsey had been delighted to get the hot potato of Ireland out of his hands, even if it had meant the withering contempt of his colleagues in the Cabinet. The news that he was to be moved to the Ministry of Education had come as a great relief to him, but his happiness had been short-lived. A week after his appointment he had awakened to find a photograph of himself and his son, Mark, splashed across the front page of a Fleet Street newspaper. SOCIALIST MINISTER'S SON AT TOP PRIVATE SCHOOL, the headline had screamed. In the photograph his son was wearing his school uniform. The article which accompanied the photo had called him a hypocrite, a tyrant who forced others to have their children educated in substandard State schools while he used his inherited wealth to have his son educated outside the system.

In a fury he had shredded the newspaper into a hundred bits. No sooner had his tantrum finished than the phone began to ring.

He had escaped to his offices in the Lord North buildings on the Embankment, but the phone continued to ring. Reporters from television, radio and the press demanded to know whether the damning article was true. He had refused to speak to any of them.

To give himself a break he had taken an old colleague to lunch at The White Tower in Charlotte Street. The lunch had been excellent, but his friend had left him in very little doubt as to what had to be done. Upon his return to his offices, he called the BBC Parliamentary Correspondent and taped an interview for the six o'clock news. The story had to be killed as soon as possible and certainly could not be allowed to continue in the papers for another day.

In his smooth, easy, intimate television style, he had dodged a few difficult questions and had then squashed the story flat.

"For those scandal-mongers who have sought to impugn my personal honesty, I have some very bad news. My son's attendance at Bruton Academy hinged upon an agreement made many years ago between myself and the present headmaster of that school. I have fulfilled my part of the bargain by sending my son there and am now free, as from the end of this term, to have him educated wherever I choose. He has been booked into Westdale Comprehensive from next term. I have every confidence that he will receive an excellent education there." He had taken the precaution of phoning the headmaster of Westdale before the interview and he had agreed to keep quiet about the lateness of the enrolment in return for receiving into his care the son of the Education Minister. "Privilege," Dempsey droned into the camera, "must be stamped out and comprehensive schooling is one of the most effective weapons in the hands of socialists." The interview had been shown later that night and the incident had been forgotten by the following morning.

Mark had at first refused to believe that his father could have done such a thing, but when the MP came to collect him at the end of term the boy had seen the guilt in his eyes. Fred Dempsey had been desperately jaunty all the way home in the car while Mark had sat in glum silence, betrayed and alone. He had wished with all his heart that his mother had still been alive. She, he concluded, would never have allowed any of it to happen.

The three-week Easter vacation had been torture for father and son alike, the boy nodding dumbly at his old man's arguments about equality and fairness, the father bending over backwards not to scold the boy for his irrational approach to the whole affair. Only once had Mark ventured to question his father about the new school.

"What kind of uniform will I wear?"

"Why, none at all. You may wear what you like. Now won't that be fun, Marksie?" It was a childish endearment that the boy hated.

Later that day, Fred Dempsey, thinking that Mark was playing in the garden, wandered into his room without knocking. The boy had been standing, gazing wistfully into the cupboard mirror, dressed in the uniform of Bruton Academy Senior School. Dempsey had soon dismissed the terrible pang of guilt that coursed through him at that moment. There was no way he could back down on his earlier decision and that was that. Mark had hated the cold, impersonal buildings of Westdale Comprehensive from the start. He had liked his fellow pupils even less. It had soon become evident that the feeling was mutual. He had been bullied incessantly, his books torn up, his clothes ripped and his glasses broken. The whole school had been sprayed with graffiti about him. The large white insulting letters stood as a constant reminder of his isolation. But he never complained to the authorities and he would have died before telling his father.

"Well, how's your new school, Marksie? Settling down all right?"

"Yes, father."

"I told you it wouldn't be so bad, now, didn't I?"

One day, Mark decided, he would have his revenge. One day he would tell his father to go and fuck himself. The school had also broadened his vocabulary.

He stood by his desk and stared around him. The thirty other children in the class were whispering, sniggering, and giving him shifty glances that told him that something special had been prepared for the afternoon, some new torture for their delight and his discomfiture.

Mark's chief tormentor, Terry Fulton, a fat boy too old for his years, slouched into the room and leaned against the wall just inside the door, fixing Mark with his sardonic gaze.

Mark felt dizzy for a moment and blinked. Not wishing to provoke another fight when he felt so odd, he looked away and opened his desk lid, whereupon the general noise of restrained mirth increased. An odd smell rose from the depths of the box-like structure and Mark, his mind still not functioning properly, poked his hand inside and felt something warm and soft. He withdrew his hand hurriedly. Sticking to his fingers was a brown substance he had difficulty in identifying. He raised his hand to his nose and sniffed. It was excreta.

He gagged and his stomach began heaving at which the other children went into paroxysms of laughter. Terry Fulton strode to the nearest desk, opened it and gave a graphic panto-mime of defecation, sending the class off into further spasms of laughter. Terry suddenly lifted a book and hurled it at Mark. It missed his head by inches and immediately the others began throwing everything they could lay their hands on. Amidst a hail of school equipment, Mark crouched down low behind his desk in self-defense, carefully holding back the tears of self-pity and desperation that threatened to overwhelm him. He had learnt from the start not to show his emotions. It only added to their enjoyment. As he remained there, hunched uncomfortably, an anger began to grow within him, a black rage he had never experienced before. He became so lost in himself that he failed to notice the arrival of the teacher and the subsequent silence of the pupils.

When he poked his head up from behind the desk, the teacher was standing by the door, his eyes weary as he looked around the classroom. He sighed and moved over to his desk, where he put down his books before turning to the class.

"I could hear that bloody racket on the other side of the street. What in God's name is going on?" The children assiduously avoided his gaze, but a boy on the opposite side of the room to Mark raised his hand.

"Please, sir. It was Dempsey, sir. He started it all."

The teacher's eyes moved slowly around the room. The class was so big that he was still unsure of names and faces after a whole term of teaching. When he had identified Mark he walked to the back of the class until he towered over the boy.

"Is that right, Dempsey, is it all your fault?"

The boy shook his head determinedly, refusing to speak.

The teacher sniffed at the air. "What's that disgusting smell?" Mark opened his desk lid. The teacher bent forward but straightened up quickly, his nose wrinkling with disgust.

"Did you do this, Dempsey?"

Although he had determined not to speak out, the anger flashed through Mark again. Why should he cover up for them? If this was the way they wanted to play it, that was all right by him.

"No, sir. It was Terry Fulton."

A shock went through the class as the teacher swung round towards Terry. "I can believe it, Fulton. You can come with me to the headmaster. Right now. I'm going to have him write to your father about this."

The boy looked terrified at the mention of his parent. The teacher had played his trump card. He knew that the old man had a violent temper that often exploded against both his wife and his son. It would mean a beating for the kid for sure, but the teacher wasn't going to feel sorry about that. The boy had had it coming for weeks.

The teacher and Terry disappeared for a few minutes. While they were gone, Mark's eyes glazed over and his breathing became shallow, but he no longer felt ill. There was excitement in his blood, and pleasure, the same tingling pleasure he had recalled from the events in the laboratory. As the feeling increased, he became increasingly remote from his surroundings. There was something he had to do, some place he had to go after the lesson. His ears pricked. Had he heard someone calling him? Yes, there it was again. But it wasn't a shout from outside. It was inside his head.

Terry returned eventually and spent the rest of the lesson leering back menacingly at Mark, but failed to elicit a response.

At the end of the lesson, the teacher dismissed the class but ordered Terry to stay behind, ostensibly to clean the blackboard, but in reality to allow Mark time to escape. The teacher wanted to avoid any chance of Terry engineering some instant revenge. Terry was in a foul and ugly mood and he glared at Mark as the boy walked up the aisle between the desks towards him. As he approached his tormentor, Mark stared directly ahead, no emotion on his face. The only sign of animation were his nostrils, which quivered as if he was sniffing for something.

As he reached Terry's desk, the fat boy stuck his leg out to bar his exit. Mark turned slowly and brought his eyes down to look at Terry. Terry stared boldly back at first, but saw something in Mark's eyes that disconcerted him. Slowly, he removed his leg without being asked to do so.

When the five minutes had crawled by, Terry, who had regained his courage in the interim, tore from the classroom, eagerly stopping other children to ask after Mark. One of his friends pointed north.

"But that's not the way he goes home," Terry shouted in annoyance.

"I know," the other boy answered, a puzzled expression on his face, "that's why I noticed him. He looked funny as well, like he was dreaming or something." Terry ran off down the street, sweating profusely, his fleshy cheeks a livid red in the hot afternoon sun.

Within minutes he had found Mark and was some ten yards behind him. Terry paused when he came upon him, stopped to get his breath, and then began to stalk his prey in earnest. He decided to wait until they had reached a quiet spot where there would be no interfering adult to spoil his plans. And what plans they were!

After he had been trailing the frail boy for several minutes, Terry noticed something odd about him. He was walking in a majestic, steady line, seemingly oblivious to his surroundings. At one point Mark veered across the road without looking as if he could just sense that there were no cars passing at that point. It made Terry feel strange, but he pressed on.

In ten minutes they had walked to within two hundred yards of the motorway. Mark turned into the churchyard. Terry, some thirty yards behind, chuckled softly to himself. The idiot was going into the ruined church. As Terry and his friends had been responsible for much of the desecration that had befallen the building in the year since its abandonment, this was most definitely home territory for him.

Mark walked straight up to the heavy oak door which provided entrance to the dilapidated building, and, as his hand made contact with it, it seemed to open in front of him without any real pressure being applied, as if the hinges had been freshly oiled. Again Terry felt uneasy. He knew the door to be stuck solid. He and his friends had often tried to shift it, but had always been forced to get in through the windows.

The fat boy cursed himself. The hour of his revenge had come and it was no time to lose his battle. He smacked a balled fist into a pudgy palm and followed Mark, slipping quickly inside the open door. The silence was eerie after the noise of the road.

All that Terry could hear as he pressed himself against the cooling stone by the side of the door was his own breathing. He screwed up his eyes and peered into the gloom which was illuminated at intervals by shafts of light jetting unevenly from the broken stained-glass windows. He could feel his nerves growing taut, the muscles of his flabby stomach tightening. His breathing became shallower and hoarser as he engaged his whole concentration in attempting to catch a glimpse of his enemy.

The light touch on his arm caused him to scream. He scuttled backwards, keeping his arm on the wall. In front of him stood Mark, illuminated in the glow of daylight from the door, his eyes wide open, glaring, his arms outstretched towards Terry.

The fat boy gulped back his fear, clenched his fists into two balls and advanced menacingly on Mark.

"I owe you something, you rotten bastard," he shouted. His courage grew as his own voice echoed, loud and assertive, around the building's hollow interior.

Mark didn't move as Terry approached. Terry drew back his fist and was about to bring it crashing down into Mark's face when something held him in check. A strange power surged from Mark's eyes, rooting Terry to the spot and bringing a numbing paralysis to his body. He stood for a moment, arm raised, like a statue in the ghostly half-light.

And then Mark smiled, drawing his lips back, exposing his teeth in a chilling grin. Terry gasped. The eyes, they were changing. Burning, glowing ...

There was a sound behind Terry. Tearing himself from Mark's gaze, he swung round. He peered once more into the darkness. Something was staring at him. He could feel it but he couldn't see it. His legs were spread wide and his arms were stretched out in front of him as protection against the unseen menace.

The shadows before him started to move, shapes flitting through the shafts of light, swirling mysteriously. Something evil was out there, he could sense it.

There was a thud. He swung back towards Mark, but the boy had gone. He saw with horror that the door had closed, ran towards it and began tugging desperately. It was stuck solid. Wouldn't budge an inch, let alone enough to let him through into the street. He pulled harder and harder. The unseen things were coming closer towards him. There was a breath of something on his back. Was he imagining it? He couldn't face turning round. His muscles bulged through layers of fat, sweat poured down his face and he began to cry, to howl, screaming for help, his cries drowned by the roar of traffic.

He took a deep breath in order to renew his hysterical efforts. In the silence he heard two sounds that chilled his blood.

Mark chuckled. It was an icy sound that crawled up Terry's back. And then another sound. Something far worse. A low, purring noise that he could hardly hear at first but which grew to a crescendo until it vibrated heavily through the deserted building, echoing ominously from the black recesses.

Terry slumped despairingly to his knees and, half-blinded by tears, slowly moved his head to peer over his shoulder.

The sight that met his bleary eyes caused a hand of fear to crush the breath from his lungs with one mighty squeeze.

The purring noises stopped and the shapes moved forward once more. Inhuman screams floated to the top of the building and out of the windows to be swallowed up by the roar of diesel trucks gearing down as they approached the motorway.

CHAPTER FIVE

Detective Sergeant Billy Crowther propped himself on his elbow and stared wearily at the phone blaring beside his bed. He glanced at his watch. The luminous dials glowed in the darkened room. It was 5:15 PM and he had been asleep for four and a half hours.

With a sigh he reached out and picked up the receiver. "Crowther," he barked. The phone chattered for several seconds.

"Dead dog? Oh, Dempsey's house. Got you. Give me fifteen minutes."

He slammed the receiver down. A body stirred restlessly beside him under the thin cotton sheets. He reached out and gently stroked the dark brown skin of the girl's shoulder. He smelled her stale perfume, pregnant with the promise of cheap pleasure and felt himself becoming excited. With a sudden movement he swung his legs from the side of the bed and stood up. He didn't have time for that.

He dressed quickly, glancing occasionally at his sleeping companion. He tried to remember her name but soon gave up. It didn't matter. He had written it down earlier in the morning in his address book. They were all the same anyway—easy lays, desperate for company, smeared with lipstick and scent, excited by the prospect of sharing their bodies with a hard copper for a night. For Crowther it was just an easy way to release tension after a tough night's work.

He moved into the bathroom, plugged in his electric razor and shaved quickly, rubbing his chin hard with the metal. At least she wouldn't steal anything before leaving. They knew better than to pinch from a copper.

He concentrated on Fred Dempsey. He knew something about his disastrous reign in Northern Ireland. Crowther's brother had been seriously wounded by a sniper's bullet on the day when Dempsey had started his talks with IRA leaders. He also remembered that he had turned down police protection and had brought in a private security firm instead, so the man was obviously a stupid bastard. And something about his kid moving to a local comprehensive school because his father had gone to the Ministry of Education. Silly business. That was about it. Hardly a complete picture of the man, but at least it gave Crowther something to start with.

He splashed on some aftershave lotion and leant forward, examining his skin in the mirror at close range. Not a bad face, he reflected. It had stood up well to the pressures with which he had been forced to live.

At the age of twenty-eight, Crowther was definitely a high-flyer. He had come south from Manchester at the age of twenty to sample the excitements of the Big Smoke. Within a year, sickened by the degradation he had seen all around him, he had joined the Metropolitan Police Force. Two years later he was working in cars and then there had been a surprise move to the CID and a chance to conduct his work in plain clothes. And then, twelve months previously, had come his promotion to detective sergeant. He still glowed at the memory of the event. A hick from the north, and he had suddenly become the talk of the Station.

That was the easy part. The hard part was never being allowed to fail. He had picked up very few friends during his meteoric rise. His northern bluntness had caused him endless trouble with colleagues and superiors alike. Up until his last appointment he had been promoted because he was too good to ignore. From now on there would be no "have to" about it. If he wanted to rise further he would not only have to keep an entirely clean copybook; he would also have to make some important friends, and fast. So he had a choice—curb his tongue and play the game, or stay true to himself and settle for a quiet career. He hadn't made up his mind yet.

He finished examining his face and then started on his hair.

He undid the knot on a small leather wallet lying beside the wash-hand basin. It rolled open to reveal an array of combs: black plastic, tortoise-shell, and steel. He picked up each one in turn and worked carefully until every curly red hair was in place. He sprayed it quickly and picked up a hand-mirror to examine the back of his head and, satisfied, moved back into the bedroom. He chose a hand-tailored, light grey herring-bone suit, a blue-and-white striped shirt and a wide floral tie.

He opened the closet door wide and examined himself once more in the mirror. The clothes, the hair, his appearance in general—it all made him feel good, made up in some way for the years of grinding poverty in a northern slum.

He turned for a moment at the bedroom door and glanced back at the bed. Another number in his little book, another phony exotic name, another body to clasp in the middle of the night when loneliness threatened to overwhelm him. He could see the twin mounds of her breasts, soft and enticing, through the sheets.

He slipped through the door hurriedly, banging it loudly behind him.

It was still unpleasantly hot as Crowther surveyed Fred Dempsey's lawn in the early evening sunlight. A faint breeze ruffled his hair above the temples. He stroked the offending locks back into place.

The bodies of the Doberman and the three cats were stretched out in front of him on plastic sheets in varying states of mutilation, ready to be carted off for laboratory examination. The three household servants stood in line by the front door as if they were waiting to receive important guests. Nearby, on the lawn, the old security guard was talking to a constable. The old man was clearly upset. Crowther walked over to him, motioned for the constable to stand aside and patted the guard on the back. "Now, come along, old son. They tell me you used to be a copper. Bet you never acted like this on a case." The admonishment worked and the old man pulled himself together.

"Sorry, sir," he choked out. "I loved that dog. It was a good 'un. You don't find many like that."

"I understand how you feel, but I've got to ask you some questions." The guard nodded. Crowther continued. "Now, the constable's filled me in on the broad events, but I'd like to hear it from you. What were you up to when all this was going on?" He nodded towards the dead animals.

The old man looked scared for an instant and glanced surreptitiously at the ground. "Patrolling the house like I do every afternoon."

"Come on, old son. Coppers make lousy liars."

The old man gave him a resigned look. "All right. I was having a kip in the kitchen. That bunch," he motioned towards the three servants, "they was off in the park, so I decided to go downstairs for a bit of water to cool meself down. Next thing I knew I was waking up in the cook's chair. I must have dozed off. I knew something was up right away—you know, the way you do—so I popped upstairs and had a look around. There was nothing wrong inside, so I went to the front door, opened it and there was poor old Wolf. He was dead when I got to him. He was a real good 'un, sir."

Crowther signaled for the constable to step forward and look after the old man and walked back to the animal corpses. Two police scientists had arrived and were poking around the bodies. They barely acknowledged Crowther as he stood over them.

At length one of them looked up. "Here, would you mind moving out of the sun and letting us get on with our work?"

Crowther shifted slightly. "Know anything about cats?" he asked, innocently.

The forensic experts looked up again, annoyed by the question. "No, as a matter of fact, I don't. I suppose you're a bloody expert," said the one who had complained about his presence.

Crowther hunched down and, pointing at each corpse in turn said, "That's a Russian Blue, that's a Siamese and that's an ordinary short-hair. Can't tell what color, though." The scientists looked at each other disbelievingly. "My father used to breed cats," he added.

"And bastards," muttered one of the men.

Crowther laughed, straightened himself, and walked over to the servants.

"And where were you when all this was going on?" Crowther addressed the butler, who had pretended not to notice the policeman's approach until the last moment.

The servant looked uncomfortable. "In the park, sir."

"And what's Mr. Dempsey going to say when he gets back?"

"He will most probably dismiss us from his employ, sir. I might add at this point that none of us would be particularly upset."

Crowther grinned. "Sod, is he?"

"Not quite the epithet I should have chosen, sir, but nevertheless a fairly exact description of the man." As if to underline his words, the gate flew open and Fred Dempsey strode into the garden.

"Who's in charge here?" he shouted.

Crowther turned to the three servants. "I'd get inside if I was you. I'll send someone in to get your statements." As the servants scuttled up the steps into the house, Crowther turned to face the angry MP.

"Who are you?" Dempsey demanded.

"Detective Sergeant Crowther, sir. Paddington Green CID."

"Where is your superior?"

"I'm handling this investigation at the moment, sir."

"A sergeant? I want someone with a bit more authority than that and I want him right now. Do you understand?"

Crowther looked hard at the man. He was all bluster, a real politician. Crowther had his measure.

"The Detective Inspector is probably out dealing with something unimportant right now, like a murder." He carried on quickly before Dempsey had a chance to explode. "As you were no doubt informed on the telephone, your guard dog has been killed. I'm waiting for further information from our chaps over there." He pointed to the dead animals and Dempsey looked in that direction.

"Good God. What happened?"

"That's what we're attempting to find out, sir. If you'd like to go into the house, I'll come and tell you as soon as we've learned anything."

He walked quickly away, leaving Dempsey furious but

powerless to do anything but obey.

The scientists stood up at his approach.

"Well?"

"Difficult to explain how it all began," said the one who had done all the talking. "The dog died of loss of blood caused by severe external injuries. Same goes for the cats, although it looks like one of them was crushed to death."

"So what happened?"

"Sounds daft, but it looks as if the dog was killed by the cats and the other way around. The only problem we've got is trying to tell how these cats got to the bottom of the garden. Something or someone must have tried to hide them there. Look at this one. It's cut in two. Couldn't have walked there now, could it?"

"No," Crowther agreed. "That'd be taking the whole 'nine lives' thing a bit far."

"Don't know about that, sir. Only one thing I am sure about."

"What's that?"

"It's got bugger all to do with the IRA."

Crowther looked sharply at the man. "I'll decide that, if you don't mind. Just you stick to the facts. Thanks anyway for the information. You can take them away now, if you've got all your samples." The men nodded. Crowther turned towards the house, furiously thinking of something to tell Dempsey. He wouldn't be too pleased at having been called away from Parliament for nothing.

The garden gate opened suddenly and a small, thin boy of about twelve walked through. It had to be Fred Dempsey's son, thought Crowther. There was a definite facial resemblance, and the fact that both had blond hair and wore horn-rimmed glasses emphasized the similarity.

The boy looked around for a moment. When he had caught sight of the dead animals, he started to walk across the lawn towards them. Crowther moved forward to intercept him and, as he came up close, noticed the dreadful white pallor of the boy's face and his discolored teeth. Crowther put out his arm. He didn't want the boy to see such a terrible sight close up. The boy brushed him aside with extraordinary force and continued to walk straight ahead as if drawn by some unseen power towards the corpses. Crowther, thrown slightly off balance, stared after the slim figure, astonished by the boy's power and worried by the glazed expression in his eyes. It was almost as if he was hypnotized.

The boy stopped in front of the Doberman. The police scientists stopped wrapping up the cats and stood back, unnerved by the child. The boy looked at the dog for a moment, dispassionately, and stepped sideways to look down at the cats. He stared at the bodies for a moment. His eyes filled suddenly with tears that burst from him and cascaded down his cheeks. His face contorted and he gave a terrible, blood-curdling shriek, his body arching backwards as he screamed at the sky.

The policeman froze at the sound. Fred Dempsey's anxious face appeared at a ground floor window and the uniformed constable came hurtling through the front door.

The boy dropped to his knees and, still sobbing, buried his face in the mess of blood and fur.

No one moved. After ten seconds that, for Crowther, seemed to stretch into eternity, the boy stood up. His face and blond hair were smeared with blood, and entrails stuck obscenely to his lips. He blinked several times in rapid succession, looked around dazedly, and then fell, unconscious, to the ground.

CHAPTER SIX

The small sports car weaved in and out of the traffic at a steady eighty miles per hour. Professor Vole, rather than look ahead at what he was sure would mean approaching death, sat sideways in the passenger seat staring at John Inglis as he spoke.

"I had been conducting experiments on the cats for about three months and, besides a certain agitation and irritability in the animals, had not got any spectacular results. However, I had a very strong presentiment that something important was bound to happen if we kept subjecting them and the bacteria to different tests. I was proved right a week before that final lecture was due to take place.

"A fresh batch of bacteria had been administered and we had put the room temperature up to ninety degrees Fahrenheit. I had to leave the laboratory to answer a phone call, and left my lab assistant, George Brewer, in charge. He was a very able man and quite capable of looking after things on his own. He had just started to reset the locks on the individual doors when I left.

"As you know, the phone is situated outside the lab door. I had just started speaking when a series of loud screams caused me to drop the phone and run to the door. When I opened it, I …" The professor stopped talking, unable to go on.

"What happened? Tell me," Inglis almost shouted.

The professor took a deep breath and continued.

"When I opened the lab door, George Brewer was lying on the floor. The cats were all over him. I was about to launch myself forward to save him when the largest of the animals, a huge brute, ripped George's throat apart in mid-scream. The animals turned towards me. I shut the door, locked it, and while I heard them smashing against it trying to get through, called the Ministry of Defence. I didn't quite know what I had done and I just wanted them to take charge of the whole thing.

"Immediately after I had phoned, I stood there by the door, listening to them moving about, and, for the first time in my life, I went to pieces. They had to put me in hospital. They found me lying on the floor, crying and shouting. It took me some three months to recover. I can still see poor George lying there to this day.

"Somehow, they managed to persuade me to carry on my experiments. I discovered that the bacteria had caused a disease which alters the very structure of the brain cells, changes the very nature of the animals affected."

Inglis, keeping the wheel of the racing car steady with one hand, lit a cigarette. On either side of the vehicle, flat fields stretched away to the horizon, the crops brown and burnt by the hot sun.

"What else did you find out? Give me all the details."

The professor sighed. "All right, John. You asked for it. As you know bacteria vary widely in terms of the amount of organisms needed for infection to occur. About two thousand organisms are needed for plague and about twenty thousand for anthrax. Even when infection has been achieved, the disease takes several days before it becomes obvious. In some cases several weeks elapse before death, and even then only eighty-five per cent of the victims die at most."

"OK. How many organisms are needed for infection to occur with your bacteria, how long before the results of the disease become obvious, and how long before death occurs?" Inglis asked impatiently.

"John, you're going to find all this very hard to believe, but try. At the most, two organisms are needed to transmit the disease." Inglis whistled softly. "The whole process takes only one and a half minutes once the necessary heat has been applied."

"Jesus Christ." Inglis's hands began to wobble on the steering wheel.

"Only five per cent of the animals I tested were immune to

the disease. The only deaths that occurred were caused by the animals themselves. Usually self-inflicted wounds sustained while attempting to escape from their cages."

"In other words, Professor," Inglis said quietly, a note of awe in his voice, "you've isolated the most deadly strain of bacteria ever discovered."

"Precisely."

They drove on in silence for a couple of minutes. "Describe the full effects," Inglis said at last.

The professor pinched the bridge of his nose between his index finger and his thumb, feeling suddenly weary. "The animals become vicious. They kill anything they can lay their paws on. Their strength seems to increase five-fold, their individual intelligence heightens to a point where you begin to think you're dealing with intellectual equals. You wouldn't believe some of the schemes they dreamt up in order to escape from Porton Down. We very nearly came close to disaster on countless occasions and they had to be kept under constant surveillance. Special guards were assigned to my project and all of them were damn glad when their tour of duty was over."

"What made you stop?"

The professor shouted in fear. He had glanced through the windscreen to see a truck coming straight for them. Somehow Inglis managed to weave away from it.

When he had recovered he continued. "During that year, I developed further strains of the bacteria to affect a wide range of animals. The reasons for doing so are obvious. Take a large city, like New York, which has millions of animals, wild and domestic, crammed into a small space. Drop in various strains of this incredibly virulent bacteria and within a few hours the whole city comes to a standstill. Conditions make it almost impossible to get the thing under control and there is no proof nor any reason to suspect that a foreign power has had anything to do with crippling the city. Repeat it in every large city in a major country and you have effectively paralyzed the nation. That's the time to bring conventional methods of warfare into play."

"So what made you give up? You must have known what they were intending to use it for from the start. You admitted that."

"They asked me to develop a strain of bacteria that would have the same effect on the human population. It's the old fighter's maxim. A man is never so easy to defeat as when you have made him angry. He gets careless, lashes out at you, while you pick your punches and turn his anger to good advantage. It's the kind of thing Muhammad Ali did to Joe Frazier. Very effective.

"That's when I decided to draw the line. Oh, far too late, I realize, but the thought of human beings undergoing what my animals had suffered was just too much for me to bear."

The professor paused for a moment, seemingly to weigh the wisdom of his next remark.

"And, anyway, the strain of bacteria which affects the cats can, in certain circumstances, affect human beings as well."

John Inglis felt physically sick with dread as he stood in the open doorway to his laboratory. The room was entirely deserted. The metal of the open cage doors gleamed accusingly in the light. One of the cages lay across the corridor. His desk was a mass of scattered papers and jagged fragments of glass. Several test tubes had fallen from the far shelf and the room reeked of stale chemicals. The vain hopes he had entertained during the hair-raising car journey from Cambridge disintegrated as he stood there.

The professor, bringing up the rear, pushed past his young companion and began swiftly checking each of the cages. Inglis followed haltingly behind him. When they had reached the far end of the room, the professor turned to him. "What was in these test tubes?"

"Nothing dangerous."

"Thank God for that."

"Well, Professor, where have they gone?" Inglis asked as Vole bent to pick up a piece of dried meat that had fallen from Mark Dempsey's white plastic bowl. Straightening himself out he answered.

"Your guess, John, is as good as mine. Probably a damn sight better, as I know nothing about this area of London. Anyway, we'll worry about that later. Go and phone the boy. He's our only lead."

Inglis scrambled for a moment amidst the heaps of paper on his desk before locating the telephone. He dialed and waited for a response.

"Can I speak to Mark Dempsey?"

"May I ask who's calling, sir?"

"No you may not, Goddammit, I've got to speak to him. Is he there?"

"I am afraid I shall have to have your name before answering that question, sir." Inglis was silent for a moment. He recognized the tone. He was talking to a policeman. He put the receiver down slowly. There was no reason for him to be suspicious at a policeman answering the phone of a Minister of the Realm, but something rankled nevertheless.

"Professor, I think you're right. We are in big trouble."

CHAPTER SEVEN

Crowther didn't even bother to knock on the door of his superior's office. Detective Inspector Jock Campbell was lying slumped over his desk, his bald head cradled by his stubby arms. Beside him stood a near-empty bottle of Glenmorangie whisky and the remains of a take-away curry. Crowther picked up the bottle and took a swig. It was damn fine whisky. He picked up the silver foil cartons in which the Indian food had congealed into greasy lumps and threw them into the waste-paper-basket. He leant across the desk and placed his fingers against the sleeping man's nostrils.

The detective snorted noisily into wakefulness and stared blearily at Crowther.

"What the hell do you want?" he croaked in his strong Glasgow accent before collapsing with a coughing fit.

Crowther waited until the spasm had subsided.

"Something strange has happened round at Fred Dempsey's house."

The old man shook his head to clear his thoughts and sat up.

"All right, give it to me."

"His guard dog's been killed, apparently by a pack of cats. I know it doesn't sound like the work of the IRA, but there's something about it I don't like."

"Well?" Campbell's voice was thick with sarcasm. It was obvious that the old man's hangover was really bad. Crowther knew that there was little point in talking to him in this state, but ploughed on.

"I wouldn't exactly classify it as high priority, but you know how touchy the big boys get when it comes to Dempsey. They don't want anything happening to him on our patch. I just thought you should be kept informed."

Jock Campbell looked irritated. "I don't see what's so strange about cats and dogs fighting. They're not noted for getting on together."

Crowther was resigned to a losing battle.

"Of course they fight, but cats rarely come off better. They either escape or get killed. It's also rare for them to hunt in packs, even when they're wild, and these looked like domestic pets. If you add all that to the fact that we're talking about a highly trained Doberman, then I think we have something weird going on." He paused for a reaction.

The old man nodded his head ruminatively. "Aye, it does seem a bit strange, right enough. Give me another half-hour's kip, then come and give me a full report. My head feels as if they're holding a Rangers-Celtic match inside." The old man crossed his arms in front of him, laid his head against them, and prepared to sleep off the hangover.

Crowther, annoyed to see his boss on the bottle again, turned quickly away before he could say anything he might regret and walked out of the office. Once outside he turned and gave the door a petulant kick. A stream of abuse followed him down the corridor.

The CID office was quiet as Crowther slipped behind his desk. Three of his colleagues were working steadily at their desks sorting through the eternal mound of paperwork. A typewriter gave off a subdued clatter from one corner of the room. A fly buzzed drowsily in front of Crowther's eyes. He thought of catching it—he had superb reflexes—but decided not to. It wasn't worth the effort.

He rifled through his top drawer, picked out a piece of clean paper and inserted it into the portable typewriter on his desk. He was wondering what to write when one of his colleagues called across to him.

"Here, Crowther, heard the one about the blind prostitute?"

"Yeah, you've got to hand it to her."

The two other policemen groaned and went back to work. Crowther typed for a few minutes, took out the sheet of paper, read it, and threw it away in disgust. It all sounded so ridiculous. He could only make the incident sound important if he drew conclusions, but there was nothing Jock Campbell hated more than guesswork.

As he sat there, he could feel a pulse of excitement running through the building. He looked around. His companions could feel it too. They had all stopped working and were hunched over their desks, waiting for something to happen.

Crowther could feel the hackles starting to rise on the back of his neck. It was always like this. He remembered the time the blacks had started rioting in Notting Hill Gate at the Carnival in 1976, and the time when the Arab potentate and his family had been gunned down outside the Royal Lancaster Hotel in '77. The information started on the ground floor where the communications center was situated, and the atmosphere of the initial shock flushed through the building in a rush. It was the smell of coursing adrenalin, the wafting odor of excitement.

The four men in the room felt it strongly. Crowther couldn't stand it any longer. He reached for his phone. As he began to dial, the door burst open to reveal Jock Campbell, his face red with booze and exhilaration.

"Boys, the Chief's just been on to me. You're not going to believe this, any of it."

He turned to Crowther.

"Cats. That's what it's all about."

Crowther gasped.

The radio announcer sipped his coffee, grimaced at the unpleasant taste, and swung his seat round to face the microphone. He watched his producer through the glass partition that sealed off the cramped, underlit studio from the control room. He glanced at his schedule sheet. The traffic report next. That was good. That meant there were only ten minutes left in the afternoon stint.

He'd been doing the show for more than a year. Every weekday afternoon between two and five o'clock, his deep Australian voice would cut through the dreadful empty loneliness of thousands of bored, neglected housewives. At first it had really meant something and it had given him a thrill of pleasure to know that he was making the day more bearable for so many people. His show, a phone-in program on WLBC—the West London Broadcasting Company—was the most popular on local radio, and it was all down to Basil Barry and his ability to make the callers feel that their opinions were really important. Even when he violently disagreed with every word they said, he managed to keep his temper. Unfortunately, the initial excitement he had felt for the job had begun to evaporate. It was just impossible to be pleasant for three solid hours each day while listening to so many stupid people. He had begun to crave five o'clock and the promise of release.

He watched his producer closely. A series of advertisements for London department stores were being aired. The producer swiveled around to face Basil at the last moment, his index finger outstretched in a needlessly dramatic gesture. Basil sighed inwardly and moved in closer to the microphone.

"And now for all you happy motorists setting off home after another day's grind, we move for a traffic report to Jim Mackay hovering somewhere above the WLBC studios. How are things, Jim?" There was silence. Basil cursed. They never got this connection right. "Come on, Jim," he started, with forced jocularity, "don't tell me you've taken the afternoon off. We can't disappoint our listeners now, can we?" He giggled nervously.

There was a terrible crackle of static and Jim Mackay's voice came over loudly. Too loudly. The engineer in the control room lurched at his control panel to change the voice levels.

"Hallo, Basil, well here we are floating up the M40 from Hammersmith to Paddington in our WLBC helicopter. It was a bit cloudy earlier on, but the sun's come out and it looks like we're in for a beautiful evening. Unfortunately this has meant that hundreds of people have been trying to sneak away from the office early to catch a bit of sun before bedtime and it's absolute chaos down there …" Basil's mind started to wander. He lived in Paddington, about ten minutes away from the studios, so the traffic news didn't matter to him. He quickly checked the contents sheet for the following day's program. He would give the listeners a trailer on forthcoming attractions right at the end of the show. Jim Mackay's voice droned on. Basil flicked through a mental list of restaurants for the evening. He was taking out a high-class lady and he'd decided to shell out a few five-pound notes to give the right impression. He decided on San Marino's—opulent, expensive and impressive. He could always stick the bill on his WLBC expenses.

"Jesus Christ!"

Basil looked up quickly. Had he heard right? Through the glass partition he could see his producer's face mirror his own amazement. He listened closely for Jim Mackay's next statement. There was another loud crackle of static and then Mackay came through loud and clear, his voice tinged with hysteria.

"I can't believe it. Something odd's happening down below. I'm getting the pilot to take us in closer. Good God! The streets are swarming with animals. I can't quite see what they are. Cats! Thousands of them. They're everywhere."

Basil jumped out of his seat as the producer flew for the cut-off switch. Had Mackay gone crazy? A practical joke? No, this was too serious. The traffic man's amazement had seemed genuine. Basil's producer signaled frantically for him to get back in his seat. They were on live now.

He spluttered for a few moments. "Well, thanks, Jim, we'll be hearing more from you tomorrow." Somehow Basil doubted that very much. "Pity we couldn't hear everything you were saying. We seemed to have a bit of a faulty connection. The general message seemed to be for you motorists sneaking home early to avoid the Paddington area." He was babbling and his mind was racing. Through the glass partition he could see the control room filling with employees from the news and administrative sections. There was a lot of shouting and arm-waving going on. Perhaps Mackay had been drunk after all. It had happened before. They'd had to cut him off the air six months previously when he started singing "White Christmas" in the middle of a broadcast, but he hadn't sounded drunk this time.

As the *Basil Barry Show* theme music welled up, Basil tore off his headphones and leapt out of the studio door. His producer turned to him as he burst through the connecting door to the control room.

"The switchboard's jammed. We didn't get him off in time. Some loonies are claiming that what he said was true." The rest of his report was lost in the general hubbub. Basil screamed for silence.

"Look, I don't want to overreact, but hadn't somebody better take a trip upstairs to street level and see what's going on. Either the guy's on acid or we're in trouble."

The producer shrugged and moved towards the door. "'Tis a far, far better thing ..." he declaimed to general laughter before exiting.

CHAPTER EIGHT

The bell rang loudly in the hot flat. Molly threw down her battered copy of the *Daily Mirror* in disgust. That was about the fifth time that afternoon. It was too hot for work but her pimp, Carlos, would beat her up if she didn't produce some money by the end of the week.

Resignedly, she picked the intercom off the wall. "Zsa-Zsa here. Can I help you?" she mouthed, chewing gum. She listened to the halting English of the man standing apprehensively at the front door of the small lodging house.

"All right, love, come in. I'm on the second floor. Just come up the stairs and I'll be waiting for you." She pressed the button to release the catch on the door and waited for the click that told her that her client had entered the building.

She walked quickly to the mirror, picked up a comb and dabbed disinterestedly at her hair, then smoothed the crumpled negligée over her firm breasts.

"Not bad for thirty-nine, doll," she muttered and strolled to the door. She listened to the feet clattering up the stairs and hoped fervently that he didn't turn out to be a pervert. She was sick of them asking to be whipped or for her to dress up in schoolgirl's clothing or leather gear. If this character tried anything funny, she'd ring for Big Tony, the bouncer.

As the feet came up to her door, she reached under her negligée and tweaked her nipples to make them stand out alluringly against the see-through material, then took the chewing gum from her mouth and threw the sticky tasteless wad into the wastepaper-basket.

There was a tentative tap at the door. She forced her

heavily-painted lips into a smile and opened it.

The Arab was expensively dressed and heavily perfumed, but short and ugly with heavy, unpleasant features that were not helped by the stubble on his chin. He had obviously been drinking and weaved slightly. She suppressed a strong urge to slam the door in his face. She had seen what her pimp could do to women and, anyway, the man might be carrying a lot of money on him. She ushered him in and put the door off the latch. They were well-protected from police interference, and it made it easier for Big Tony to gain access if he was needed.

"What's that, love?" The Arab was speaking to her. "How much? Oh, we'll think about all that later, shall we? Give me twenty to start with. As a deposit. No, D-E-P-O-S-I-T. Get it? Good. Now go over there and take your clothes off, there's a good boy."

When she was sure he wasn't looking, she slid the two crisp ten-pound notes between the sheets of the Gideon bible by her bed. It was the last place they'd think of looking for money in a whore's bedroom.

Her client was ready, standing embarrassedly in the middle of the room, his hands draped nonchalantly in front of his body in an attempt to conceal his private parts. Molly undid the clasp on her negligée, whisked it off, sat on the bed, and patted the soiled, grey sheets beside her.

"Come on, love, don't be shy. It won't be that bad."

The Arab took a few halting paces forward and then flung himself on top of her. She lay back, bored as he began to writhe and grope. One thing was certain, she thought, the man was no expert, but at least the session would be short if not altogether sweet. She was just calculating how much she could get away with charging him when he suddenly stopped moving and gave a little squeal.

"Well, you're a speedy one," she muttered and deducted ten pounds from the figure she had previously arrived at. He hadn't been in the room for more than five minutes.

The man squealed again, more insistently this time and then he began yelling. She felt him become heavier and then he was screaming at the top of his voice. Molly tried to move but his weight had become fantastic. Something brushed past her leg. "Shut up!" she shouted. She'd been with a lot of perverts, but this was a new one on her. She tried to shift her head, but his hands clasped at her face, momentarily blinding her. She began to hit at the Arab. Where was Big Tony? Her own shouts of fear began to mix with her client's.

Then she felt him start to slither off her body, his manicured nails digging into her flesh. Something was pulling him off and he was resisting. Big Tony? She wrenched her head free of his grip and looked down.

Her mouth opened wide, but no sound came from her throat. Her eyes bulged from their sockets and she froze solid where she lay.

The cats had dug their talons and teeth into the Arab's back and were systematically dragging him towards the door, his hands clasping uselessly at the receding bedclothes. The Arab slid off the bed with a thud and Molly could hear his flesh rasping against the wooden floorboards through his continuous screams. As his head disappeared around the door, she could see his eyes staring upwards, sightless in agony. There was a trail of blood and strips of flesh from the bed to the door.

Molly came to and bolted for the door in a desperate attempt to shut it. She heaved her shoulder against it but something was stopping the door from closing properly. She shoved hard, fear aiding her strength, but it still wouldn't move. From outside she could hear the Arab's gradually weakening screams. Looking down, she saw a cat's paw, crushed and bleeding, acting as an immovable wedge to her actions. Slowly the door pushed back against her. There was no way she could stop it from opening.

The old lady shuffled through the gates of the small, green park, her precarious progress aided by two gnarled rubber-tipped sticks. Her tatty silk dress furled slightly in the faint breeze. A group of young boys raced noisily past, punting a football. They shouted something rude at her which she pretended not to hear. She stopped every five or six feet to regain her breath. The years had taken their toll and she no longer looked forward to the summers, especially if they were long and hot. It had been so different in her youth: crinoline dresses, amusing cocktail parties in lush private gardens and the welcome attention of admiring, handsome young men. But she had been famous then, one of the belles of the London Stage, her beauty adorning many an Edwardian light comedy. It had been a long time since anyone had paid her any heed, but every now and then some old soul would come over to her and ask if she was who they thought she was and that always made her day. Imagine, she used to think to herself, people remembering you after all this time, and, on those occasions, she would go back to her disheveled bedsitter and get out the photograph albums and indulge in the powerful drug of nostalgia.

Apart from that, this was her only pleasure: a daily trip to the park to feed her birds and to look around the elegant London Square where she had once owned a complete house and where Ivor and Noel and all the bright young things had come to call on her.

She was pleased to find her regular bench empty and maneuvered herself onto the wood with a sigh of relief. She sat for a few minutes, panting slightly, her hand fluttering over her chest. When she had recovered, she looked down to find her faithful brood clustered expectantly round her feet.

"Good morning, fellows," she crooned in her faint, high-pitched musical voice, scrambling in her pocket for the shriveled brown paper bag. Her long, arthritic fingers poked inside, bringing out the morsels of dried bread which she threw to the eager pigeons. Each piece produced a flurry of wings, and a running battle between the larger birds had soon started.

"Morning, dear. Lovely day." She looked up to see the policeman smiling at her. She gave him a practiced coquettish grin and he strolled on.

When the bread was all gone, she leant forward slightly, tipped the bag upside down, and showered breadcrumbs over the birds' heads.

The sound of shrieks and squeals interrupted her reverie. On the far side of the square, the children that had passed her earlier were rolling around the ground and chasing round in circles. What were they up to? She screwed up her eyes, but it was no use. She reached into her handbag for her spectacles. As she searched, the cries became more insistent. When she had got them on, she looked up only to have her line of vision obscured by pigeons, their wings beating frenetically, rising from the ground in front of her in some obvious panic. When they had gone, she looked down. Staring up at her from the ground was a cat with long bat-like ears, a live pigeon clutched between its extended jaws, rustling wings bulging horribly from either side of its mouth. The bird struggled desperately. As she watched, the cat silenced the bird by clenching its jaws together. Blood dripped steadily from the pathetic grey carcass. The cat began to munch.

The old lady, outrage welling inside her, grabbed one of her sticks, ignoring the pain that shot through her fingers, and prodded fiercely at the cat. The animal swiped a paw annoyedly at the object but refused to budge. With a great effort the old lady hoisted herself off the bench, onto her legs, and took two agonizing strides forward. Something dug into her leg. She looked down. Another cat was staring up at her, a hunk of bloody flesh disappearing into its mouth. Blood was pouring onto the ground. There was a large, jagged hole in her leg, just above the ankle. She shrieked and hobbled forward, the cat attacking her persistently. In the distance she caught sight of the children once more and this time she could see what was happening to them. Her feet caught in a stray tree branch and she careened forward, her skull hitting the concrete pathway with a loud crack. Mercifully, she was dead before the cats got to her.

Kurt crashed back into his chair, the loud music throbbing through his head. His brushes with reality had become less and less frequent since he had escaped the stifling provincialism of his small home town in Germany. One day, after a brutal beating from his steelworker father, he had packed his bags and, under cover of night, had set off for Amsterdam. As countless magazine articles and television programs had told him, that was the place to go if you were a young person in search of excitement and experience.

He had spent several weeks there, floating from commune

to commune in a drug-induced haze. Soon he had developed a cocaine habit which his limited resources and the generosity of his new friends would simply not support, and he had turned to petty thieving, luring old men into dark alleys and snatching handbags. He had even tried to sell dope to Dutch schoolkids and, at this stage, the police had decided to intervene. Only the amorphous nature of the city's underground life had allowed him to escape one rainy, wind-swept night over the sea to England.

In no time at all he had met up with a group of renegade European youngsters and was safely ensconced in a squat in Paddington. To his amazement he had found that the police had no legal right to evict them from the house. He and his friends had all signed on at the Labour Exchange and, by a process none of them was able to explain, were receiving large sums of money from the government for not working. To Kurt, Britain was paradise on Earth.

By the simple expedient of inviting a pusher to live with them the group had made sure of a steady supply of any narcotic they desired. The day normally started with a couple of joints of marijuana followed by a late-morning snort of cocaine. In the afternoons they might trip on LSD and, if they were going out in the evenings, sniff some amyl nitrite or take some speed.

On the few occasions when none of these drugs could satisfy him, Kurt would tie a rubber tube around his arm, hold it in place with his teeth, drawing it tight until his veins stood out like a relief map, and inject himself with heroin, but even his hazed mind realized the dangers of continued practice.

It was late afternoon and Kurt had just popped his second acid tablet of the day. It was just beginning to take effect and Kurt could tell that it was going to be a good trip. The opposite wall began to buckle, bending in the middle. A bird in a poster flew out from the wall, seemed to circle the room lazily and flew back into the picture. The music came across the room to him in solid waves, the heavy beat shuddering through his body. The smoke hanging in the air curled and writhed into different distinguishable shapes and the rough texture of the carpet under his hands merged through his skin.

It was a marvelous trip. The best he had ever had. The other people in the room gazed at him in vague interest. His dealer was trying to persuade them to take some of the stuff and they were waiting to see if Kurt was going to have a good trip.

To Kurt, his friends were undergoing a fascinating variety of kaleidoscopic transformations, at first merging into the furniture, becoming a part of the beds and chairs on which they sat, and then turning into animals, huge lumbering bears and then resting lions. The shapes became smaller and began moving towards him. At first he couldn't make out what they were and he didn't really care. He settled back to enjoy the wildly changing sensations and stared up at the ceiling which seemed to move down to meet his gaze, lowering itself until it was almost touching his head. He didn't like that at all, so he shifted his gaze back to the room.

The animals were still moving over the carpet towards him, coming in droves. They were cats, he could now see, and he smiled. He liked cats.

He watched dispassionately as the first animal reached him and trapped his hand in its jaws, its teeth sinking slowly downwards until they had punctured his skin. Its small, triangular head moved back and forth in rhythmic shakes and soon Kurt's hand was a shredded mass of red, bloody meat, bones staring, white and naked, up at him.

There was no pain as they began to work their way up his body, ripping and chewing each square inch of flesh until the surrounding carpet had become a gooey pool of seeping blood, and Kurt didn't worry about it at all. It was all experience. It was only when they had reached the upper part of his chest that he began to worry. The trip was turning bad and pain was beginning to filter through to his chemically-numbed mind.

He saw the claw coming down in a lazy arc. It dug straight into his cheek, grinding against the bone. Suddenly everything became clear. He screamed and, in the distance, he could hear the sound mingle with similar horrified rantings. He tried to move his hands to fend off the cat going for his eyes, but it was too late. The teeth ripped into his eyeball. With his one good eye he stared down the length of his body. Between the writhing bodies he could see himself, his limbs like lumps of freshly-ground hamburger meat. With every last reserve of strength that he possessed, he tried to shift his torn body, but it was no use. As the full horror of it all dawned on his mind, his life extinguished, receding into blissful nothingness like a dot on a fading television screen.

Gerald Franklin angrily shoved his hand onto the car horn and left it there. He did it for two reasons. He hated women drivers, especially when they pulled in front of him without signaling, and, more importantly, he liked to draw people's attention to the gleaming Daimler limousine.

For most of the day he was forced to drive around wearing a silly little chauffeur's cap and bum-freezer jacket while an assortment of fat businessmen and American tourists issued imperious orders from the luxurious comfort of the back seat. But as soon as Gerald had finished his daily stint for the hotel chain, he would drive around the corner, tear off the cap and pull on a smart sports jacket. Then, during his half-hour drive home to his flat in Marylebone, he became a king, pretending to himself and spectators that he was a wealthy businessman, or even an eccentric aristocrat, driving his own car. Each stare of envious hatred that he received from pedestrians and fellow drivers gave him a thrill, but best of all was when he pulled up at the traffic lights beside another expensive car. He would glance with a practiced laconic half-smile at the other driver to let him know that they belonged to the same club.

The lady driver nervously pulled the Mini Cooper onto the side of the road to let him pass. Gerald let his hand, which was resting nonchalantly out of the window, rise in a disdainful gesture of thanks and increased speed. In the distance he could see a group of commuters standing at a bus stop. He would give them one of his looks as he passed. That should really put them in their place.

Something brushed against his arm and he shook it casually. *Damned cyclists*, he thought, but the contact came again. He looked sideways at the open window and yelped, lifting his foot off the accelerator. It was a bad mistake. The cat hanging to his arm lunged at his face and the area in front of his car became an ocean of animals. The car wheels bumped as they rolled over the massed bodies.

Gerald fended off the attack and shook his arm to loosen the grimly-clinging beast. It made another dive for his face, this time making contact with his throat, teeth sinking inwards, forcing his head back. The car almost stopped and bodies flew in at both open windows. Gerald let go of the steering wheel, his limbs thrashing out in wild, spastic movements. As his foot smashed repeatedly against the accelerator, the car lurched forward in a crazy stop-go motion like a remote-controlled tank.

The commuters had turned and were rushing hysterically up the road to escape the animals and the automobile, pushing and trampling over each other. As the insane car came abreast of the running group, it collided with a bus coming in the opposite direction, veered off its side in a screech of metal, and ploughed into the confused crowd, scattering and throwing bodies in every direction before smashing into a shop window.

A burly man in an ill-fitting pin-stripe suit launched himself out of the vehicle's path, tumbled on the ground and was on his feet in an instant. He gazed around in bewilderment. The cats were all around him. Across the road stood a pram. A woman was trying to get to it, but every time she came within reach she was swept backwards by the onrushing animals and finally disappeared for good under the flood. The man began to stagger across the street, his feet rising higher and higher with each progressively more difficult step. What he would do once he got to the child, he didn't know. He just knew that he had to try and save it.

When he had got to within ten yards of it, the pram tottered and crashed over sideways. He caught a glimpse of white cloth and a pair of terrified, button eyes and then it was covered in a threshing melee of fur. The man stopped in his tracks. A black cat, noticeably larger than the rest, leapt at his groin, sinking its teeth into the loose material around his crotch. The man lashed at the animal but the very force of his blows caused him to fall over.

As he lay on the ground he could see people jumping from

the smashed upper windows of the double-decker bus and then his eyes locked with those of the black cat. Its jaws gaped for a ghastly instant before its teeth rammed straight through the flesh of the man's nose and crunched into the hard knuckle of gristle underneath.

CHAPTER NINE

The phone calls hit Paddington Green Police Station in a rush. Hysterical, frightened voices, raw with terror, wailed down the line. At first the police telephone operators had received the calls with their usual detached calm, but soon the very number of them and the horrifying nature of each one began to tear at their nerves and the fear and tension began to crawl through the building.

As Crowther listened to Jock Campbell's brief description of events, he knew that he had been right. The behavior of the cats in Dempsey's garden had not been normal and the dead Doberman had been a warning, a sign, but what could anyone have done about it? He took some comfort from the thought as he raced behind his boss down to the underground car park. The old man had decided to look at things for himself. "You can't get a true picture until you've seen it up close," was another of his favorite sayings. If he'd had any time, Crowther would have argued with him. If Campbell's report was true, they were going out to offer themselves as bait to a pack of crazed animals. Crowther could think of nicer ways to go.

As he swung the car onto the street, he said to his superior: "I know it sounds stupid, Guv, but all this, if it's true, it sounds like a plague, like something out of the ..." his voice trailed away. It sounded preposterous when spoken aloud.

"Aye, son. I know what you mean. It's like something out of the Bible." The old Presbyterian Scot seemed to relish the idea. "Like Sodom and Gomorrah. Reckon our little patch could make those towns seem pretty tame by comparison."

Crowther nodded as he raced through the traffic. It was

exactly what he had been trying to say.

There was a sudden hush in the crowded studio control room as Basil's producer skidded to a halt just inside the door. He stared at them wildly for a moment, gasping for breath.

Basil ran over to him. "What's wrong?" he shouted.

"Mackay was right." There was a sudden rustle of indrawn breaths.

"Rubbish. You're having us on," laughed one of the crowd.

The producer screamed at him incomprehensibly. It was several seconds before they could get him to speak coherently. "This is no joke. The whole place is swarming with them. When I got to the front, the doorman had just locked the doors. I could see them through the glass. Hundreds of them crushing in against it. Across the road I caught sight of the new secretary, you know, the one that started here yesterday. She was just standing there open-mouthed. In seconds they reached her, dragged her to the ground and where all over her." He hunched over and began sobbing.

"What then? What did you do then?"

The producer looked up at Basil. "We dragged two of those six-foot metal filing cabinets and got them across the doors just as the glass splintered. You can hear them scraping away, but I don't see that they can get in. The doorman's holding them in place."

"What's in the cabinets?" asked Basil.

"Nothing."

The Australian rushed out of the door and careened down the corridors of the underground studio.

The doorman was leaning with his back to the cool metal, his cap pushed to the back of his head, the sweat running down his face in steady rivulets.

As Basil ran up to him, he looked in his direction.

"Sir, I seen plenty in the war, but I ain't never seen nothing like this. I just hope to Gawd it's all a nightmare."

"Sorry, mate, it's all too real. How many of them are there?"

"Bloody hundreds. Look out sir!"

Basil looked around worriedly. On the ground in front

of him lay a cat, its skull crushed, brains spewing onto the linoleum.

"Who did that?"

"Your friend, sir. One of them got through the doors before we got these filing cabinets up. The gentleman just brought his foot down on it, but not before it got me."

Basil looked down at his legs. The thick black material of the doorman's trousers was ripped in several places and blood was seeping through the gashes. While Basil stared, he felt a faint breeze against his cheeks, filtering from the slight crack between the two cabinets.

And then he noticed the sound. In the distance he could hear human beings in pain, but the noise that held his attention was nearer, quieter, more insidious. Clawing and scraping. It became louder. Suddenly, with a screeching noise that shivered up Basil's spine, the metal began to crack in several places at once and talons burst through, gleaming. The small punctures grew with frightening speed until, just below the doorman's outstretched left arm a whole leg appeared. Barry watched in horrified fascination as a pink nose poked through a fresh crack next to the doorman's right leg. The cat pushed and tore, the metal edges of the cabinet digging straight through its cheeks leaving red bloody scars, until its whole mutilated head was through. Barry stared into its eyes. They were lifeless. The air had been crushed from its lungs by the weight of numbers cramming from behind. The head disappeared back through the hole and a new face took its place, only this time it was very much alive. Its jaws gaped and from its gullet escaped a lunatic, lust-filled rasp. Basil could feel its hot, fetid breath from five yards away. Its lips drew back over its fangs in a grimace so malevolent, so mindlessly evil, that Basil cried out in terror.

Through his fear he suddenly became aware of a human voice shouting at him. The doorman was in a wild panic and, as Basil watched, dumbstruck, the cabinets began to topple forward. Basil jumped and brought his shoulder crashing against the unsupported cupboard just as it tottered dangerously. As he righted it, a cat's paw snaked out of the metal and drew a ghastly, livid gash through his cheek. Basil yelped and brought a fist smashing against the offending limb. It severed and dropped to the ground at his feet.

The metal was beginning to buckle and Barry watched in total horror as the doorman lurched forward and the cabinet he had been supporting fell on top of him. The cats began to sweep over in a single tidal wave. Basil began to pray out loud. This was surely the end.

Then a line of human beings, startling in its ferocity, met the cats head on. Basil leapt forward and turned to join them as his own cabinet toppled. Hearing the noise from the control room, the crowd had armed itself and now met the cats with metal chair legs, wooden clubs, even foot-long shards of glass. The men and women shrieked and screamed as they stomped and stabbed, falling on the invaders with a crazed wildness until the animals turned and began to run. The crowd followed relentlessly, those without weapons bringing their feet crunching onto the backs of the retreating foe. When the last of the living cats had scrambled back over the cabinets, Basil's colleagues rushed to push them back into position.

The ensuing silence was eerie. Basil stood back and surveyed the carnage. Amidst the piles of dead cats lay three bodies, dead, blood pouring from deep wounds. The doorman had been crushed to oblivion. Others were hunched over, tending their wounds. One girl sat on the floor, holding her hands over her torn eyes, moaning in pain. That and the occasional gasp for breath were the only sounds in the room.

From the corridor leading to the studios, a cat's head appeared and then disappeared. Basil, with a yell, took off after it. Within seconds he had caught up with it and crouched close behind, still running, flaying at it with his bare hands. The cat somehow managed to squirm and wriggle out of his grasp until they came to a dead-end corridor.

The animal turned calmly and gazed up at Basil. Its eyes were wary but the fight still flickered in them. Basil, his whole body shaking with rage, advanced, stopped some feet short, hunched over, and waited for it to make its move. Without warning, the cat made straight for his face. His hands, guided by fury and hatred, grabbed its slender, twisting neck and began squeezing.

He watched with pleasure as the animal's eyes began to bulge outwards, and, as he held it inches away from his face in order to see its dying agony at close range, he began to laugh, louder and louder, until it had become an hysterical cackling.

He went on squeezing long after the beast was dead, and only when his companions came to find him did they get Basil to release it. They led the shaken announcer back to the studio. He still had a show to do.

Crowther brought the car to a screeching halt. Crowds were racing out of the top of Praed Street and the parallel road, Sussex Gardens, and running blindly across the Edgware Road, their faces etched with terror. They kicked and pummeled each other in sheer panic. Crowther and Jock Campbell forced open the car doors. As he stood there, Crowther could see several unfortunate souls being trampled underfoot. He shivered in anticipation. What could have caused such fear?

Campbell disappeared amidst the bodies and Crowther chased after him, fighting hard against the shifting, human barrier in an attempt to keep his boss in view. The people hit out at him as he battled against the current. "You're mad... Run while you can... They'll kill us..." they shouted. His gut had knotted into a hard knuckle of fear by the time he had caught up with Campbell.

The old copper was standing at the end of the road, staring in astonishment down the length of the wide, tree-lined avenue. The scene that met their eyes resembled, Crowther afterwards remembered thinking, a Hieronymus Bosch painting, a graphic depiction of Hell itself.

The street was awash with writhing animal bodies, a troupe of cats indulging in an obscene but fascinating dance of death. Cars and buses had been brought to a halt, swarming with cats with partially chewed limbs hanging from their mouths. Crowther saw an arm rise grimly from one side of the road. It shook briefly in agony and then fell limp before being covered by the beasts.

Crowther could feel the nausea rise up in his throat. The cats had halted about fifty yards from the end of the avenue, momentarily satisfied by their spoils, but Crowther felt that they would begin moving again at any moment.

As the two policemen watched, the doors to one of the terraced houses opened about forty yards from them, and a line of children, no more than six or seven years of age, ran down the steps into the street. Behind them came a stout, middle-aged lady. She was obviously a teacher, the kind of charming old battle-axe that Crowther remembered from his own infant school days. The children, emitting a chorus of high-pitched wails, looked confusedly around them when they reached the pavement. Crowther could hear the teacher yelling at them above the din. A black child, slightly larger than the rest, must have understood her, for he took the lead and began racing, a small tot clinging to his arms, up the street towards the coppers, his floppy plimsolls pounding the tarmac.

Crowther, instinct getting the better of him, began running towards them, shouting encouragement. A small group of cats farther up the road had begun to turn their attention towards the children, staring after them in a way that chilled Crowther. He ran past the kids, waving them on until he had reached the end of the straggling line. He was about to turn after them when he realized that the old lady wasn't around. He looked again. Her enormous, matronly bosom heaved as she thundered towards him. The waiting cats chose that moment to make their move. About twenty of them broke away from the main group and speared towards the teacher. In seconds they had moved in and she had fallen. They were all over her.

Crowther let out a roar and, lifting his legs almost to his chin, covered twenty yards in an instant. Ignoring the snarling jaws that bit deep into his hands, he plunged into the shifting heap and grabbed the old lady's arm. With a fantastic effort he began to haul her away. He didn't even know if she was still alive. The cats continued to attack her and began leaping at Crowther's unprotected head. Lashing claws flashed by, centimeters from his eyes.

As he weaved and ducked his head, he could feel the strength draining from his limbs. It was hopeless, but, just as he was ready to lay down his burden—how could she be alive?—and run for it, strong hands gripped his arms. He turned in amaze-ment. A uniformed policeman pried his grasp from the teach-er's arms and, with a shove, sent him reeling up the street in the direction of safety. He needed no persuading and broke into a gallop. Three other policemen passed him going towards the cats. As he ran, he saw a line of cars drawn across the top of the street acting as a metal barrier. Jock Campbell was standing waiting for him. "Bloody fool," he muttered as Crowther raced up. His boss grabbed him by his jacket and hoisted him over the nearest car bonnet before clambering after him.

Crowther got to his feet. The policeman had managed to get the teacher off the ground and two of them were supporting her from either side. The front of her cotton blouse was soaked in blood and her arms and face, where exposed, were a mass of cuts.

Bringing up the rear was a third policeman, his truncheon raining blows upon the heads of the furious animals.

Crowther saw the body of the fourth copper lying some ten yards behind the retreating group. If he wasn't dead already, he soon would be.

Some dozen cats were still in hot pursuit as the policemen reached the line of cars. They threw the old lady violently across the bonnet and vaulted over themselves. Their companion started to follow, but a warning cry from Crowther made him stop. Floating through the air towards him, almost, it seemed, in slow motion, was one of the largest cats that Crowther had ever seen. The constable, alerted, saw it in time and met the animal with a heavy swipe of his truncheon. The cat shrieked and thudded against the policeman's shoulder on its way to the ground. The copper staggered under the blow and fell to his knees. He was dead in seconds. The cats went straight for his jugular vein. As the blood spurted over them, Jock Campbell leaped onto the car bonnet and, drawing a .45 revolver from his armpit holster, began to pump bullets into the hideous gang. The cats turned and flew back to join their already-advancing comrades, moving menacingly up the road.

The young man's companions retrieved his body and stretchers arrived to take him and the teacher away. The children gathered around as she was lifted from the ground. She managed a weak smile of assurance before passing out.

When he turned back from witnessing the touching scene, Crowther was shocked to note the close proximity of the line of cats. No more than thirty yards and moving in. Jock Campbell was leaning in through his car window, yelling into his intercom.

"Hope it's a direct line to God," Crowther mumbled to no one in particular.

Crowther turned his attention to the area behind the cordon of cars. At least three hundred people were looking on, some in their cars, some perched on the automobile roofs, others just standing in the road. After the initial panic they had begun to seep back, afraid to miss anything.

"Get out of here, you crazy bastards," Crowther bellowed and slowly they began to drift away.

He turned back to the cats. Twenty yards. He looked down at his hands. They were badly cut. He placed them in either pocket of his jacket to try to stem the flow of blood. When he looked up, the cats were no more than fifteen yards away. He was so frightened he could feel his bowels roiling, but he couldn't run, not until Jock Campbell issued the order, and he still had his head stuck in the car window, still yelling orders into the intercom.

A familiar, sawing sound filled Crowther with relief. He turned round to see the fire engines ploughing through the parked cars, bulldozing them out of the way. He glanced back at the cats. A dozen yards, no more. The engines lined up, three abreast, directly behind the cordon of cars. The firemen, helmets gleaming in the sun, moved busily over the bright warm red surfaces of the machines, unravelling lengths of hosepipe, setting up their positions.

The cats were five yards away. There was a quiet, sinister determination in their progress that made Crowther's knees buckle. Campbell was still yelling, his voice rising to a crescendo as the animals came up to the car. Campbell could see them quite clearly through the window.

Crowther could stand it no more. He reached into the automobile, grabbed his boss and physically dragged him away, refusing to stop until they had reached the safety of the fire engines. They both turned to look.

The cats had begun to climb over the roofs of the cars when the jets of water hit them. A forty-yard wall of solid liquid spewed forth from the eight massive hoses. The animals stopped dead with the initial impact and began to slip helplessly back over the tops of the cars. The watching crowd began to cheer at the sight, but the roars stopped in their throats as the animals reappeared. Crowther could hear the firemen cursing as they began to spray the line once more.

This time the cats were ready for them and began to seep under the vehicles where the water jets were not aimed. As soon as the trajectory of the hoses lowered to meet the new threat, sweeping the encroaching bodies back under the car wheels, a flood of cats launched themselves over the car roofs, this time meeting no resistance. It was too late to stop them. The firemen began to drop their hoses.

As if acting upon some prearranged signal, the animals who had previously approached with the hunched patience of lions, moved into top gear, covering the yards to the engines with the speed of cheetahs.

Crowther yelped with fear and staggered back from the engine behind which he had been crouching. Something knocked him to the ground.

CHAPTER TEN

Crowther looked up, dazed. The line of paratroopers was advancing steadily, knocking aside anyone in their path with professional detachment.

The air was suddenly full of the sharp crackle of machine guns. The cats halted, juddered and seemed ready to fall back. The guns blasted forth in one continuous volley. The cats stood their ground, heedless of companions dropping dead around them. They occupied an area five yards in front of the line of parked cars. Others hunched on top of the automobiles. A seething, multicolored blanket of fur was visible between the hoods of the cars. The front line coldly assessed the situation as the continuous hail of bullets tore into them and then, incredibly, they started advancing once more, cautiously at first and then with increased confidence. The troops began slowly to edge backwards, their heavy-duty army boots scraping against the road surface.

There was a momentary lull in the firing and, as the crackle of the guns started up again, the cats pounced, their composure gone, snarling and spitting furiously at the troops.

Crowther gasped. This was the last hope. Once through this line, the whole of London lay at their mercy, defenseless against one long, bloody rampage. He heard a dull explosion and rapidly scanned the scene to discover its source. One of the cars in the protective line had burst into flame, fire pouring from its engine and racing through its insides. Hideous belches of black smoke curled upwards from the wrecked vehicle and, before the cats or the troops had had time to react, the blaze had crept to the next car which exploded with a dull boom. The cats milled about in confusion. One of the soldiers, catching on that the petrol tank of the first car had been ignited by a stray bullet, began strafing the rest of the automobiles. Soon his companions had joined in, a steady barrage of lead thudding into the motors. Within seconds the whole line was ablaze, a readymade funeral pyre for the animals on top. Flames licked out at the cats on either side, frying them where they stood. The heat rapidly took care of many more, asphyxiating them in seconds. The few who were far enough away to escape the inferno ran forward blindly to be met by the deadly accuracy of the machine guns.

From where he stood, Crowther could feel the overpowering heat singeing his body and clothes, but he couldn't have cared less. The air was filled with the noxious smell of burning petrol and with the wild, screeching sounds of the burning cats.

A heavy, black pall of whirling, writhing smoke hung over the scene, obscuring everything behind and in front of the cars. Crowther held his breath. The guns were silent. What would they see when the smoke cleared? A line of cats waiting to surge forward once more, this time with no obstacles in sight? Slowly the flames began to die as the automobiles burned themselves out. Crowther peered into the gloom.

Suddenly, a gust of wind blew up and the smoke cleared for an instant. Crowther could make out piles of incinerated bodies and the air was heavy with the cloying odor of charred meat. All the cats in sight were dead. The animals left alive in the holocaust had retreated. The humans had won ... for the moment.

As a steadier wind started to blow and the smoke lifted completely, Crowther could hear the sound of cheering behind him. He turned. From all directions, out of shop doorways, from behind cars, from back alleys, people were pouring forwards to acclaim the troops. The soldiers stood in a firm line as the crowds began to swarm around them.

Crowther strolled up to the dead cats. As he stood there an officer came up beside him, and kicked one of the corpses. "Well, that should be the last of them," he commented smugly.

Crowther shook his head in sharp disagreement.

"I'm afraid we've only seen the first."

Basil Barry, a clumsy dressing strapped precariously to his
bleeding cheek, was back at the microphone doing the most
important broadcast of his career. This was one show he
couldn't afford to fluff.

"Ladies and gentlemen in the Paddington area, please listen carefully to me." He reached for a glass of water, took a
sip and continued. "This is the most important announcement
you're liable to hear for a long time. Please stop whatever you're
doing and listen to me." He had to get their attention without
conveying his own panic. "I must make this clear from the
start. This is not a hoax and it is not an advert. You must understand that. When you hear what I have to say, please do not
panic. Remain calm." If they weren't listening now they never
would. Where would he start? Right in the middle. "Animals
are roaming the streets of Paddington and parts of Bayswater.
Something has happened to our cat population. They have
turned wild. If you live within the area bounded by Edgware
Road, Sussex Gardens, Bayswater Road and Queensway, please
follow these instructions. If you are indoors, lock all doors and
close all windows. Place all heavy furniture in front of all possible entrances to your home or office. Even if your apartment is
situated at the top of a building, follow this advice." He gulped
at the water again. His voice was beginning to shake and that
was no way to inspire confidence. "If you are listening to this
broadcast out of doors, move inside at once. If you are close
to home, make your way straight there. If that is not possible,
gain entrance to the nearest building. I cannot overstress the
seriousness of the situation. Your lives are in danger. There are
two ways of safeguarding yourselves. Remain calm, and listen to my instructions. Keep tuned to this station for further
developments."

He moved back from the microphone as the studio reporter,
armed with fresh news from the police, slipped into his vacated
seat. Basil walked through to the control room and spoke to his
producer.

"Never let me hear anyone call local radio boring again.
Now, someone get me a drink—and none of that piss-warm

British beer." For the first time since the attack there was laughter in the small room.

Crowther slumped into his chair and stared for several moments at the pile of paperwork on his desk. Two unsolved murders, a recently discovered cache of heroin, and a series of jewel thefts to be dealt with. It was strange how insignificant they seemed now.

He lit a cigarette and leant back in his seat, exhaustion beginning to seep through his limbs. The police force had prepared him for many sights: the results of a brutal axe murder; the bloated remains of a suicide dragged from the Thames; a dead junkie, arms covered with suppurating sores. Crowther had seen and accepted all that, but nothing had prepared him for the scenes that he had just witnessed. Perhaps, he reflected, a veteran of the trenches in the First World War would have taken it in his stride. One thing was certain—Crowther could not.

His phone rang but his mind was so occupied and numbed that he didn't notice it for nearly thirty seconds. He reached out and picked it up, wincing with pain as his injured hand grasped the receiver. It was the desk sergeant. There were a couple of men downstairs claiming that they knew something about the cats. The Chief Inspector had suggested that Crowther speak to them. He told the sergeant to send them up to a nearby interrogation room and stood up wearily. Troops had ringed the area, police were standing by from every station in London, all television and radio programs had been cancelled so that news of the events could be transmitted continuously and his precious boss was suggesting that he interview loonies.

On his way to the room, he dived into the bathroom, examined his hair in the mirror, began combing it and then, disgusted with himself, broke the comb in two and threw the pieces into the corner.

The two men were pacing nervously up and down the small, windowless room as Crowther entered. He walked silently to the naked wooden desk that commandeered most of the available floor space and sat down. The two men had stopped pacing and were looking at him anxiously. He motioned for them to sit down as well and studied them for several seconds. One was a youngish, dark-haired man with a drooping moustache. Crowther detected something faintly alien in his manner. The other was a tall, gangling middle-aged gentleman with the unmistakable demeanor of an academic. They certainly didn't look like the usual lunatics, the professional confessors that accompanied every big case. And there were two of them which was also unusual.

"All right, gentlemen," Crowther began, "so you know all about the cats?" He glanced sharply at each of the men in turn. They both stared back and began to speak at the same time. Inglis's sharper American tones rose above the professor's.

"Yeah, that's right, and you can remove that sneer from your voice. We're damn serious and we're not mad. We started this whole mess and we're here to see if we can help clear it up."

Crowther gawped in astonishment. The professor took over from his young companion. "I can vouch for everything he says. My name is Vole and I'm Professor of Microbiology at Cambridge University. You can check up on me later." He continued quickly, not allowing Crowther time to interrupt. Briefly he told the policeman the whole story, being careful to minimize his pupil's guilt.

When the professor had stopped, the room was silent for almost a minute. Crowther knew he was telling the truth. He had known it from the man's first sentence. There was about him an air of honesty and respectability that suggested he had better things to do than hang around police stations concocting fantastic stories.

"This disease, can it affect human beings?"

The professor thought for a while before answering. "Yes, it can, but the circumstances necessary for successful infection are so rare as to be negligible."

"Just one more question before we get serious. Why the hell should I believe you?"

Inglis jumped up from his seat and leant menacingly across the desk. "You stupid bastard," he shouted, "haven't you been listening to him? Does he look like the kind of guy who would come here and lie to you?"

Crowther raised a hand to silence him. "All right. I believe you. Now tell me, what can be done?"

The two men grew silent. Crowther repeated his question, a hint of annoyance in his voice. Perhaps they were hoaxers after all.

The professor began to speak, but halted, seemingly in the middle of an internal argument and then said: "I know that there is a way to alter the behavior of the animals but I can't put my finger on it. It's there in the back of my mind. I just can't isolate the thought. You'll have to give me time, I'm afraid."

Crowther sighed. "Look, sir, we don't have any damned time. We can't afford to wait for your brain to start working. That might take days. The little bastards could be all over London before you come up with the answer."

The professor gave him a sad smile. "I'll admit that it's very frustrating, young man, but there it is. I might be the only hope you've got."

Crowther stood up suddenly. "All right, wait here." He ran through the door and down the corridor to the Chief Inspector's office, brushed aside the half-hearted complaints of his dragon-like secretary, and burst into the room. A number of annoyed faces stared up at him. He had interrupted some kind of conference.

Chief Inspector Andrews rose from behind his desk. "Crowther, blast you, who told you to come bursting in here without knocking? Get out or I'll have you suspended."

Crowther decided his only hope was to stand his ground. "Chief, this is too important to wait. I have to speak to you. Right now."

The Chief Inspector, a thin, ascetic-looking individual in his early forties, strode quickly to the door and stepped into the outer office, leaving Crowther to follow in his wake.

After dismissing his secretary he turned. "Make it fast, Sergeant, and make it good." Crowther took a deep breath. "I've got two men in Interview room D17 that claim they're responsible for what's happened to the cats. One of them is the Professor of Microbiology at Cambridge University. He seems quite genuine."

The Chief's face went a dangerously purple color. Crowther raced through the story and, by the time he had finished, Andrews had regained some of his composure.

"Do you seriously expect me to accept this rubbish?" he asked coldly.

Crowther decided to make one last bid for credibility: "Look, sir, I'm laying my career on the line here. The least you could do is give me a chance. If you have connections at the Ministry of Defence"—Crowther was on safe ground. He knew that Andrews had important friends there—"ask them about the experiment. If they say that nothing of the kind has been going on, then, all right, I'm wrong. I'm sure you won't forget the fact."

Andrews gave him a wry glance and moved over to the nearest telephone. He dialed rapidly, asked for an extension, and began speaking slowly and deliberately. It was obviously some prearranged mode of speaking, a code to be used when conversing on an open line. Crowther hoped that the message was getting through.

"All right, phone me back. I'll be waiting." Andrews gave his number, replaced the receiver and walked to the window. Crowther followed him. They gazed out in silence for several moments. The window afforded a panoramic view of the rooftops of Paddington, but nothing much could be seen of the streets themselves.

"Wonder what's happening down there now," the Inspector mused. Crowther decided it wasn't a question requiring an answer.

The phone rang. Andrews picked it up and listened for several minutes. "Really, now isn't that interesting? Oh, blast security. Two men have just walked in off the street to tell us all about your precious little project. I've also got two representatives of your Ministry sitting in my office at this very moment and they seem quite ignorant of all this. When this is all over, someone's head is going to be on the chopping block. I just hope it isn't yours."

Andrews slammed the phone down and turned to Crowther. "Bring your friends into my office. This meeting should be fun."

For no reason at all that anyone could think of, the cats disappeared. Not a slow, steady retreat, but a sudden and complete disappearance. The troops rubbed their eyes in disbelief, the helicopter pilots flew in low over the roofs but there was not a live animal to be seen. Bundles of mutilated corpses, severed limbs, and pools of blood littered the streets as the troops began to surge forward, their heavy boots picking a careful course through the dead and dying. The whole scene took on an unreal aspect in the drowsy redness of the early evening sun. It was 6:48 PM. A stiff breeze had begun to blow.

CHAPTER ELEVEN

The Savoy Hotel lobby was crowded. A party of Germans had just arrived and were making a loud fuss over their room arrangements. A gaggle of American businessmen dressed in bright-colored sports clothes gathered around the ticker-tape machine. It held their attention for a few minutes before they strolled off to the American Bar, shaking their heads.

A youngish man in a black tail-coat and pin-stripe trousers nodded cordially at them as he walked in the opposite direction. Mr. Loyola, the Reception Manager, was making a hurried patrol of the lobby to make sure that it contained no snooping reporters. He kept checking his watch nervously and glancing towards the main entrance. As he walked he checked off each face against his mental photographic file of guests. Only two did not fit. One had the unmistakably scrubbed, severe look of the successful British tax lawyer and the other belonged to a pretty young Asian prostitute waiting for her New York theatrical impresario date to appear. Loyola knew all about him and did not mind in the least. Nothing disconcerted him any longer. A few months previously, he had been surprised on several occasions to come across a gaggle of young boys attempting to get up to one of the rooms. The Arab potentate responsible for the invitations—which had been accompanied by offers of lucrative remuneration—had been asked to leave. He had not paid his bill, which had been in the region of seven thousand pounds. Loyola had been most put out, but it had been worth the money to protect the hotel's excellent reputation. Loyola made it his business to know as much as possible about his guests' affairs, as much for their own protection as for his own. Most of

London's high-class crooks and con men had been through that lobby during his time and he was proud of the fact that most of them had been chased away. Unless it was obvious that the guests knew who they were dealing with, a discreet word was placed in their ears and, since most of the Savoy's customers were regulars, they had learnt to trust Loyola's judgment.

As soon as he had made his tour of inspection, Loyola moved directly to the front doors which were hurriedly opened for him by an obsequious porter. He strode out just as a black Rolls Royce limousine swung in from the Strand and purred down the narrow entrance between the Savoy Theatre and Grill.

The doorman bustled forward as the car came to a halt and opened the near-side door. Loyola stepped forward, a pleasant, welcoming smile on his face, but almost gasped in astonishment as the towering figure of Duke Inglis levered itself out of the wide back seat onto the pavement. The man was grotesquely and clumsily disguised. He wore an outsize velvet fedora, a straggling false moustache that threatened to fall off at any moment and a full-length black cloak that swished around his ankles. He accepted the Reception Manager's outstretched hand, entirely covering it with his massive paw, and winked conspiratorially.

"As my secretary no doubt explained, I'm travelling incognito. Hope there aren't any of those damn reporters hanging about," he said, accusingly.

Loyola assured him that there were none and hustled him quickly across the lobby. All conversation stopped as soon as the big man entered and the crowd of people stood and gawped at the unlikely apparition. When he had passed through, there were pockets of laughter and general argument as to whether the stranger had been Orson Welles. At least the senator's disguise had worked, even with some of his own countrymen.

Loyola ushered the big man into the riverside suite that had been prepared for him. Inglis walked eagerly through the magnificent sitting room, bent to run his hands approvingly over the rich, plush chair-coverings, nodded with satisfaction at the well-stocked table of drinks that had been provided for him, and stared out of the broad, full-length windows up the river towards the Houses of Parliament.

He nodded happily. "Looks like toy town, but I love it just the same."

Loyola coughed quietly and Inglis turned.

"I trust that everything is in order, sir."

"Oh, sure. Just see to it that nobody knows I'm here."

"We will do our very best, sir." He bowed slightly and walked quickly to the door. As he walked up the long corridor towards the lifts, he clucked in disapproval. He had read somewhere that Inglis was likely to become the next president of the United States. How could the Americans elect a man who enjoyed dressing in silly costumes and playing the fool?

Inglis gave the porter a heavy tip, waited for the grey-suited minion to disappear, and hastily tore off his unseasonable clothes before submerging his body in a cold bath.

Afterwards he sat, swathed in a toweling robe, in front of the window. The disguise had been fun. It had reminded him of amateur theatricals at Harvard. But he hadn't expected the heat. The last time he had visited London he had been up to his ass in snow. As he gazed out of the window the sun still shone brightly, large and red.

"Crazy country," he murmured.

He got up from his chair and walked to the television set, selected the BBC button, and settled back to watch some of the fine British television his countrymen were always being asked to emulate. A newscaster's face flickered into outline. Duke leant forward to put up the volume.

"… and in the wake of the cats' disappearance, as swift and inexplicable as their arrival one and a half hours earlier, troops are combing the area. Behind them are the ambulances to take care of the wounded. So far, casualties resulting from the terrifying attack have been estimated as high as three hundred and at least three times that number wounded." Uneven, hand-held camera footage replaced the reporter's image. A few mutilated bodies were shown before a soldier's restraining hand obscured the view. The cameras switched back to the reporter. "I have beside me here Lincoln Andrews, Chief Inspector of the CID at Paddington." The camera shifted slightly to include the tall, gaunt figure of the Chief Inspector. "Tell me, sir, do we as yet know what caused the situation, and, secondly, what is going to be done about it?"

"Well, to answer the first question, no, we don't as yet know what caused this unfortunate attack. However, scientists are working on the problem at the moment and we should have an answer fairly soon. As to your second question, we are evacuating everyone from the affected area within the next few hours. Tents are being erected in Hyde Park. We are quite prepared for this sort of emergency and full facilities are available for coping with the crowds. I would like to appeal here and now for everyone's co-operation. We would like to complete the operation before nightfall, for obvious reasons. We would ask people not to bring any of their possessions with them. I am sure that it will only be a matter of days before they're allowed to return to their homes."

"But how," the reporter continued nastily, "do you know that if you don't know either what caused the holocaust or where the cats have gone to?"

The Inspector shot the reporter a sharp look.

"I am quite certain that the animals will be traced. Our reports suggest that there were at least two thousand of them involved in the assaults. It would, I assure you, be rather difficult for such a large number of animals to remain in hiding for a prolonged period." The camera swung back from the obviously annoyed policeman to the reporter. "Well, that's the report on the latest situation, so, from Paddington Green Police Station we hand you back to Bill Johnson in the newsroom."

Duke was perplexed. Cats? Attacks? His driver had mumbled something about a necessary detour coming in from Heathrow. Had this been the cause of it? There was something else that worried Inglis in the middle of the bizarre affair. Paddington. He had heard of it before and not just in connection with its station. No, the place held a more recent significance for him.

He struggled out of his seat and bent to pick up his suit jacket which he had carelessly tossed on the floor. He rummaged through the pockets and pulled out a slim scrap of paper with an address. He mouthed the words. So that was it.

He rammed the paper into his dressing gown pocket and, having located the bell for the waiter, pressed it and kept his finger there until the man had appeared. He asked the nervous servant to explain the cat situation to him. He listened, fear mounting, as the waiter talked.

"Get me a car," he barked. "Not a limousine, something less conspicuous and send the valet along immediately to open the rest of my bags."

Fifteen minutes later, the car, a sleek blue Jaguar, was stuck in a major traffic jam, with the senator fiddling nervously in the back seat. "Driver, what in God's name is the hold up?"

"Well, sir, the roads are jammed with people trying to get to see the cats. It's been on the telly, see, and everyone's talking about it. Wouldn't mind seeing them myself."

The senator made no reply. He lit a Havana cigar, a luxury that life in the States could not provide, and began puffing furiously. The driver surreptitiously opened his window to allow the heavy blue smoke to escape.

Inglis was worried about his son. Genuinely worried. Even he was surprised at the depth of his emotions. He had never been all that fond of the boy and had rarely missed him during his four-year absence. Their relationship, which had been quite healthy until John entered his teens, had been destroyed by the suicide. Duke had always known that the girl had been the cause of all the ill feeling between them. The old man had teased the girl for years, wondering out loud how he and his wife could have produced such a plain child. In part, it had been real concern for her that had prompted his tactless comments. He had wanted her to take more pride in her appearance, smarten herself up, take a greater interest in boys. At one stage, he had even offered to pay for plastic surgery.

But more important than his interest in her welfare had been his own annoyance at not being able to offer the girl as a sacrifice in some politically useful marriage. After one particularly stormy session at the dinner table, made even more unfortunate by the presence of guests, the seventeen-year-old girl had fled from the room in tears, chased by her father's voice balling for her to come back and take her medicine.

As soon as the guests had departed, John Inglis, then four years younger than his sister, had gone up to comfort the girl. Her room had been empty, but there were signs that the medicine cabinet had been rifled, and several pairs of stockings roped together on the floor had given the boy an unpleasant sensation. Coming out of his sister's bedroom, he had noticed the door to the attic standing open. The room had not been used for years. Perhaps the girl had ascended the stairs to find solace amongst her childhood toys but John did not think it likely. The girl's unattractiveness had led her to concentrate on her studies and she had, early in her life, forsaken all childish pursuits.

John had mounted the stairs slowly and had slipped noiselessly through the partly open door. He had hardly had time to comprehend the full horror of the vision that greeted him before his father, who had been following close behind, had pushed him roughly out of the door, locked it from the outside, and had run downstairs to telephone for a doctor friend capable of making out a death certificate with the minimum of fuss. It would have proved a serious blow to Duke's career to have had the incident written up in the newspapers.

After the small, almost desultory funeral, John Inglis's attitude to his father had changed radically. The boy had begun to refuse all offers of fishing trips and vacations in the mountains. He would no longer accompany his father on tours of the state and would feign stomach aches to get out of attending the political parties that were so much a part of his home life.

At first Duke believed that the child was just reacting morbidly to his sister's death, but it had soon become obvious that John had figured out his father's total culpability in the demise of the girl. Sometimes, when reading a newspaper or watching television, Duke would glance up, the hairs rising on the nape of his neck, to discover the boy staring at him with an expression of malicious hatred.

The few years that followed before John's request to attend Cambridge University in England had been frosty and unpleasant, and when the boy had come to his father with his plans for leaving the country, Duke had found it difficult to hide his relief.

The boy's stiff, unemotional departure had been followed by a few short, clipped letters, then a few ungarnished requests for money and, finally, silence.

Duke had not been unduly worried. He could probably face life without his son. Disinterest was usually the fate of fathers in a world which no longer adhered to the old values. He had shrugged away the loss. Anyway, it had made it easier to forget the sight of his daughter swinging obscenely from that attic rafter, her bloated face glaring at him in accusation. But then had come his political advancement. A long, careful lifetime of planning and plotting was, it seemed, about to be rewarded with a crack at the White House.

As soon as the dream of becoming the Republican Party's presidential nominee had become a reality, Duke had remarried. His first wife had died in a violent automobile accident while returning home in the early hours of one morning from a nymphomaniacal binge. A semi-truck with faulty headlights had veered across the road towards her own swaying vehicle. The truck, which was never found, had suffered only a slight dent. Mrs. Inglis had been decapitated. Duke had been silently thankful.

No sooner had his campaign amongst his fellow Republicans got underway, however, than the whole ugly story of his daughter's death had resurfaced in a radical underground newspaper. Hints and innuendoes had immediately begun to fill the major media.

Duke had launched an investigation into the source of the story. It had come from England. From a Cambridge University students' magazine. Duke had hired detectives to track down his son five minutes after receiving the information, but John had proved an able fugitive for more than a year. The boy had been sent down in his first year of postgraduate research for certain political activities and nothing had been heard of him since. All his mail to the university was forwarded to a friend who had proved quite impervious to the mixture of threats and bribes offered by Duke's investigators.

Duke had needed the boy for two reasons. Firstly, it was good to have a family around you during a campaign; it warmed the hearts of your supporters, while the absence of "loved ones" usually led to a number of embarrassing questions. Secondly, the boy had to be gagged. He had too much dirty information on his father to be allowed to run loose shouting his mouth off. If the media got to John first, they would have a field day. Duke simply could not afford the publicity. But those two motives for the foolhardy and reckless scheme to track down his son had been joined in his mind by a third while watching the television broadcast in his hotel room. Something that Duke had never counted on. When there seemed some chance that his boy might have died, pangs of loneliness, self-recrimination and fear had entered the old man's soul. His only son, his one remaining child, might have died without his knowing, without his even caring. Duke had suddenly realized that, more than anything, he wanted to see his son again, wanted to hold him in his arms like a little boy and tell him how sorry he was for everything that had gone wrong, for his lousy childhood, for his lack of affection, for being deprived of his sister.

The old man had been running for many years from the confrontation, and now found himself desperately eager for it. As they waited in the traffic jam, tears began to fill his eyes for the first time in many years. For the first time since his daughter had died.

CHAPTER TWELVE

The whole area was clean. The troops had swept through it three times, checking each room and basement. Three hundred and eighty-two corpses had been found, and nearly three times that number were being treated for wounds and shock. Of these, at least thirty were adjudged to have lost their sanity.

Several jeeps were traversing the area. In one of them sat Crowther, Inglis and Professor Vole.

The young American was in a state of extreme agitation, realizing that everything he was seeing—the dead bodies, the blood, the frightened, wounded people being led from their homes—was all the direct result of his own experiments. "I did all this. I killed them," he muttered softly from the back of the car. The professor tried to calm him down, but was feeling little better himself. He knew only too well that he carried the weight of the responsibility. He had isolated and developed the bacterial strain in the first place. He had uncharacteristically begun teaching the principles of his experiments to his students without working them through to the end. He had worked for the government for a year developing the poison. In his long career, he had never had his faith in the power of science questioned in such a sharp, clear way. He turned away from Inglis. He was in no state to give comfort to the young man. All the phrases he could summon into his mind seemed devoid of meaning.

"Well, Professor, what now," Crowther turned around from the front seat.

"Young man, I wish I knew."

"Well, at least hazard a guess. You must have some idea." The professor was silent, still engrossed in his reflections.

Crowther could feel the anger welling up inside him. "Look, isn't it time that you two stopped feeling sorry for yourselves and started thinking about these people?" He gestured around him. "Personally I don't give a damn who started all this. I just want to make it go away." The professor looked guiltily into the young man's hard, pragmatic eyes.

"You're quite right of course. Give me a few minutes to think about it." He lit his pipe and sucked noisily.

Crowther turned back to stare out of the jeep's windscreen. The battle with the cats in Sussex Gardens had all seemed quite unreal. But now it was different. The mutilated corpses, the strained faces of the people who had been locked in their houses while the cats had raged past their front doors—this felt only too real.

The jeep moved slowly past an ambulance into which a young child's body, ripped and gaping, was being carried.

Crowther was determined to get these bloody cats. It was personal now, like all his cases. It was no use thinking of them as the unfortunate results of an unfortunate experiment. Each of these cats was a psychotic killer. Thousands of Jack the Rippers swarming over his patch. Jack the Ripper had got away. The same thing wasn't going to happen with these little bastards. Crowther was slightly ashamed as he felt the thrill of challenge course through him.

"What's the temperature?"

Crowther was startled by the professor's question.

"I haven't got a clue. Why do you ask?"

"Well, I've been sitting here with a mass of fanciful notions running through my head. It is very difficult to explain why thousands of animals should react as if with one mind. I mean, why should they all decide to go to ground at exactly the same time. Certainly the cats are behaving with an atypical herd instinct and there is the possibility that there are certain animals acting as leaders who might have given a signal, but I would prefer a more reasonable explanation for the synchronicity of their movements. So, I thought, if the temperature caused their madness in the first place, might it not hold the clue to their present low profile?"

"In what way?" asked Crowther. Even Inglis had awakened from his reverie and was sitting forward eagerly, listening to the professor.

"When the temperature drops sufficiently, perhaps the aggressive instinct is defused while the herd instinct remains. It is early evening now. The sun has gone behind the buildings. It can't be more than seventy degrees, whereas it was over ninety earlier in the day. That's the thing that was at the back of my mind. Now that it has surfaced, what do you think of it?"

Crowther thought for a moment. "I think you could be right, Professor, but why didn't you find all this out while conducting experiments for the government?"

Vole shot him an annoyed look. "I was at that stage searching for traditional antidotes. Scientists can be fallible, you know."

"Yes, I had noticed," Crowther remarked, his voice laden with sarcasm.

"…so please cooperate with the army and the police in their attempts to clear the area. I will be joining you in Hyde Park straight after the show. Those of you who are still listening, please leave your homes and make straight for the Park. The streets are quite safe at the moment. Facilities are ready for eating, sleeping or anything else you might feel like doing. This is Basil Barry signing off, hoping to be back on the air with you soon."

He ripped his headphones off and subsided onto the table in front of him. He had just undergone a straight five-hour broadcast with a twenty-minute break to do battle with the cats. The wound on his cheek was throbbing and he felt totally drained.

The WLBC studios had been evacuated except for himself and his producer who was hastily switching off all the equipment in the adjoining room.

The *Basil Barry Show* theme tune came to a halt and the air was silent. Basil slipped a weary arm from under his head and rummaged in his pocket for a cigarette before remembering that he had given up smoking a month previously. Well, he had earned one now. He got up from the table, stretched his legs, and walked unsteadily through to the next room to scrounge one from his producer.

They looked at each other as he walked through the door. Basil motioned for a cigarette and was handed one. The two men sat down in the ghostly peace of the dead radio station. Basil drew greedily on the cigarette before collapsing with a coughing fit. When he had regained his breath there was a new sound in the room. A scraping, scuffling noise, like mice in a skirting board.

The two men looked sharply at each other, checking that neither of them was responsible for it. It grew louder, closer. Were they imagining it? The day had placed a great strain upon both of them.

"Can you hear it?" Basil asked.

"Of course. I thought it might be in my head."

"So did I."

They rose from their seats and began looking around. Basil opened the door that led to the main part of the studios but there was no sound from that direction. It was either coming from underneath them or… The two men swung round just as the wall began to buckle. *There shouldn't have been anything there,* Basil dimly thought. The studios had been dug straight into the ground. There were no adjoining basements, no water pipes, no tube-train tunnels. Nothing. Just earth. The wall strained in towards them. Basil had seen a film of a dam bursting once. It was just like that. Cracks appeared in the brickwork and widened and then the wall burst open like a split water balloon and a sea of fur flooded into the room. The two men had hardly any time to react. The producer was overwhelmed in an instant. Basil grasped the handle of the door and yanked it towards him, but the cascading waves of animals shut it again and knocked him to the ground. He couldn't breathe. He opened his mouth, but it was blocked by a wall of fur. He could see nothing. There was no pain. The animals weren't attacking him. He was just being suffocated to death. His brain began to swim crazily. He was floating down a river in a boat on a lazy afternoon, the sun warming him, and he was falling asleep. His lungs sucked inwards in a last desperate attempt for air, but there was none.

Basil Barry and his producer lay dead in a tomb of living animals.

The senator stood shouting at the policeman. The copper had had a hard day and now he had to contend with this mad American screaming at him about his son. He sighed.

"Look, sir, be reasonable. I can't let you into the area. No one's allowed in. I don't care who you are. My orders are quite explicit. No one is allowed through and that's that. All the residents are being evacuated into Hyde Park until this thing is cleared up. I suggest you go there. Everyone should have got there by about ten o'clock this evening. That's about," he glanced at his watch, "an hour and a half away. If your son's alive, he'll be there. Now please move along. I can't allow you to hold things up any longer."

Duke turned angrily away. He had seen the tents being erected in the Park as his car had crawled up the Bayswater Road. He would go to them and wait for John. Even if his son turned around and spat in his eye, it would be worth it just to see him alive again. He pushed brusquely through the straggling lines of stunned refugees.

At the first entrance he came to a policeman who was taking down everyone's name and checking them off against a residential list.

"Officer, I'm looking for my son, John Inglis, Eighty-Nine Westbourne Terrace."

The policeman looked down his list. "No one of that name listed here, sir."

"There must be. I know he lives there."

"Which flat, sir?"

"Number one."

"I have a Mr. Glissin listed under that address, sir."

"Yeah, that's him."

The officer looked skeptical. "Officer, please, I haven't got time to explain now."

"And I haven't got time to listen, sir. Mr. Glissin hasn't come through yet. Try the next entrance along." Having had no better luck there, Duke entered the Park, walked through some trees and made his way towards the huge canvas structures which were slowly filling with people. Inglis visited each of the tents in turn, peering into every haggard face as he passed. The people stared back at him with frightened, haunted eyes and, as he searched, he heard the full horrific story in a hundred snatches of conversation.

When his tour had produced no results, he moved to the center of the makeshift camp, strolling through piles of military armory, food, and chemical toilets and approached a harassed official plowing through a mass of documents in the darkening light.

No, the man didn't have a record of a Mr. Glissin entering the camp. Yes, he did have a record of the dead, and three quarters of the corpses had been identified. No, his son was not listed and neither was he amongst the wounded.

Duke stumbled from the camp, untouched by the suffering he had witnessed, concerned only for his son. He was exhausted. He could do no more that night. The blue Jaguar was waiting for him. He subsided into the back seat and told the driver to return to the Savoy. The whole of the West End of the great city was chock full of cars full of people eager to witness the calamity at firsthand. Inglis sneered at them as he passed in the opposite direction. At least he had an excuse. What kind of pleasure could they possibly get out of it?

Perhaps he would find his son tomorrow. As a survivor of many election campaigns, he had learnt never to relinquish hope.

Fred Dempsey opened the door to the bedroom quietly and stood for several minutes staring at his son. The nurse had cleaned the blood from his face and he had been given a strong sedative. The child's breathing was steady and the bedclothes shifted steadily with the slight movements of his chest. Fred moved over the carpet towards the bed, stood over his son for a moment and tentatively stretched out his hand to pat the boy's smooth brow.

"Poor kid," he muttered. He had been drinking for several hours since the shocking incident in the garden and had subsided into a state of maudlin self-pity. With all the deep pleasure of a religious fanatic, he had been wallowing in his own guilt. "I haven't been a very good father, have I?" he whispered. "Well, I'm going to make it up to you from now on." He smiled down at the child. He was beginning to feel better already. The first thing to do was to take the boy away from that dreadful school. He would think of some way of dealing with the media. Anyway they had more than enough money. He could retire if he wanted to. Move to the country. The child would be happier there.

Dempsey stroked the boy's hair away from his eyes and began to move his hand back from his face. With lightning speed the boy pounced, his eyes blazing, as his jaws opened and his white teeth sank straight through his father's hand. Dempsey stared for a moment in total disbelief and then, with a sharp yell, balled his other hand into a fist and brought it crashing down on his son's temple. He hit again and again, but nothing would shake the boy. The boy's jaws were clamped so tight that Dempsey was sure that his teeth had met through the flesh and bones. A mixture of saliva and blood began to dribble down the boy's chin.

The policeman, who had been left at the house, burst through the doorway and started hammering on Mark's skull with a truncheon until his jaws finally relaxed their tenacious grip. The child, bludgeoned into unconsciousness, subsided back onto the bed. Fred Dempsey, choking back tears of disgust and shock, walked quickly from the room, clutching his injured hand at the wrist, blood pouring from the gaping wound down his forearm.

They sat in five main groups, staring blankly ahead, their subdued eyes glinting occasionally in the shafts of early evening sunlight. At the head of each placid group sat an animal, larger than the rest and entirely black in color. The five black generals surveyed their troops.

The only sound in the vast, echoing building was a soft, low purring noise that ebbed and flowed in steady waves.

The five battalions were arranged in a vast circle, in the center of which was a vacant space where the bare ground was illuminated by ghostly, red sunlight. The animals were waiting for something to enter that space. One by one, the five leaders strode to the center of the circle, their fur shimmering in the natural light, and set up a soft, plaintive mewing that rose eerily upwards into the cavernous vaults of the room. There was a human quality to the sound, like a child crying for its mother across a wasteland. When each had finished, it stood silent for a moment before padding back to the head of its section. Each time that the ritual had been completed, it would start again.

As the evening drew to a close, the ranks of the animals grew larger as more of them appeared, seemingly from the very foundations of the building. The newcomers moved silently into each of the five groups, as if an allotted position had previously been decided. The cats already in the assembled groups paid no attention. Only the eyes of the leaders flickered over the proceedings.

Finally when there had been no additions for almost half an hour, the five black cats moved in unison to the center of the circle and set up a moaning chorus that floated out onto the night air. Then they were silent, waiting.

CHAPTER THIRTEEN

The conference room was uncomfortably hot and filled with smoke.

The Chief Inspector brought the meeting to order. The dozen men around the table slowly settled down as he rapped his fist on the table.

"Gentlemen, I apologize for the heat in here. The air-conditioning system has broken down. I suggest you remove your jackets and loosen your ties. We might be in here for quite some time." During the general disrobing that followed his suggestion, Andrews looked round the table to make sure that each of the organizations involved in the operation was equally represented. Two from the Home Office, two from the Ministry of Defence, two from the Army, two from the Greater London Council (Andrews wondered how they had managed to get themselves invited) and two from the police (Crowther and Jock Campbell—Andrews noted with surprise that the old copper was completely sober). The odd men out were John Inglis, Professor Vole, and Andrews himself.

Andrews cleared his throat. "Let me start by stating the situation as it now stands. As far as we can tell, the whole area affected by the cats has been evacuated except for three hundred soldiers and one hundred police officers. These men are armed with a variety of weapons in case the cats should reappear during the night. In addition, the area, which is spotlighted and patrolled constantly by helicopters, is ringed by a further two thousand soldiers who are prepared to move in at once should further incidents occur. It is their job to keep the people out and the cats in." The Chief Inspector paused and took a sip of water.

"Estimates of the numbers of cats involved range from three to ten thousand. I think we should keep the upper figure in mind." He looked round the table for agreement. Several heads nodded. "So that takes care of the area itself."

"Not quite," interrupted an Army colonel. "You forget that one of the buildings is still occupied. I refer, of course, to the hospital, St Mary's. I'm afraid that moving all the sick people proved too much of a task and, anyway, the other hospitals in London are not equipped to take such a sudden rush of patients. Damned bad planning, if you ask me. Anyway, we have another contingent of three hundred troops surrounding the buildings. They should be quite safe."

Crowther thanked him and continued. "Facilities have been provided in Hyde Park to house the evacuees, almost seventy thousand in number, I have been told. The people are obviously distressed but seem to be bearing up remarkably well under the strain."

"Now, as to our immediate plans. The troops will continue to search the area during the night. The cats have obviously gone to ground somewhere in here." He held up a map of Paddington with four heavy black lines drawn on it forming an approximate square. "Obviously they are somewhere underground. All the buildings within the lines have been thoroughly searched several times. We have local historians out with the troops pointing out entrances to underground tunnels. The bad news is that there are at least two hundred that we know of and, apparently, numerous ones that have been totally forgotten. We are concentrating on the main ones. Still, I would rate our chances of finding the little blighters before daybreak as fairly good.

"Now, the next question is, why did the animals disappear in the first place? Professor Vole here thinks it is directly related to the temperature. We checked with the meteorological office and they vanished as soon as the temperature fell below seventy-four degrees Fahrenheit. So, if we don't discover where they are hiding, we'll get them as soon as the weather warms up tomorrow morning. Our main aim, however, is not destruction, but containment. According to my, admittedly, flimsy grasp of the scientific facts, this disease that drives them mad spreads like wildfire. There are at least several million cats in the London area. I would prefer not to think of the consequences of them all becoming infected."

"Excuse me." All heads turned to look at Professor Vole. He looked immensely old in the glaring lights that hung around the table. "My hypothesis is based on guesswork. Does the Ministry of Defence bear out my theory?"

The two civil servants looked nervously at one another before one of them spoke. "Yes, Professor, we do indeed. Tests made after your regrettable decision to abandon the project indicate that the animals can be controlled by lowering the temperature sufficiently. We were unable to establish an upper limit."

Andrews nodded. "Very well. Let's turn our attention to the most important question of all. How are we going to stop them? Gas them? Poison the streets? How?"

The man from the Ministry of Defence raised his hand to gain their attention. "Neither gas nor poison are sufficiently effective for us to risk their use. There is also the dangerous possibility that any gas might spread further afield than originally intended—a change in the wind, for instance, might lead to regrettable results. Poison, I am informed, is altogether too clumsy a method."

There was silence around the table for nearly a minute. The Army colonel spoke suddenly in a bluff, loud voice. "Fire."

There was a slight gasp. One of the council representatives, a short, stocky man with a florid complexion and rimless glasses, rose majestically from his seat.

"The town is like a tinderbox. There hasn't been any rainfall for three weeks. The fire department is stretched to the limit. Two hotels have been razed to the ground in the past few days. I am here to represent the interests of the community. I shall brook no suggestion of using a method that might lead to the wholesale destruction of property. In fact, if such a motion is passed, I shall go straight to the media with the whole story."

"Sit down, you pompous little fool," the Army colonel shouted in stentorian tones that took away the fat man's bluster. "Now you've talked a lot of sense, I'll give you that, but this is a state of emergency. If I so much as suspect that you intend going to any newspaper or television channel with this story, I'll place you under military arrest. Understand?" The councilor gulped but remained silent.

"Good. Now just remember that the Army's in charge here. Oh, thanks for running this meeting, Inspector, but let's just remember that what we say goes." Andrews blushed angrily. "Now, we're in the middle of a war here. Certainly the enemy is a little unconventional, but no stranger than those yellow devils we faced in Malaya." He kept tapping the table to emphasize his points. "There's no use going after your communist insurgent when he's gone to ground. Won't do at all. You wait for him to make his move. Takes away the element of surprise, of course, but you make sure that you've got something up your sleeve that he doesn't know about."

He paused for a moment and stared around the table to make sure that he had everyone's attention. Satisfied, he continued.

"That's why I said fire. So far these animals have met bullets and water, but what destroyed them, eh? Fire, but from an unusual source. They won't be expecting us to let them have it front on, if you see what I mean. When they come above ground tomorrow, we'll be waiting for them with hundreds of flamethrowers."

The councilor, who had regained his composure, interrupted. "And what about people's houses? The whole place'll go up in bloody flames."

"Yes," continued the colonel. "I do take your point, old boy, but either you want to get rid of these animals or you don't. No choice, I'm afraid. Strong medicine. Anyway, you're being awfully pessimistic. We'll be backed up to the hilt by fire-fighting equipment. We'll hit 'em in the open, away from the houses." This time there was no resistance to his plan.

Andrews spoke. "So the plan is to wait for the cats to show themselves and then go at them with flamethrowers, no matter what the damage to property. Does anyone disagree?"

"I do, and, furthermore, would like that recorded." Andrews looked at the councilor wearily.

"Very well." He looked around at the other men. Crowther

and Jock Campbell shook their heads. So did Vole. Inglis seemed about to say something but changed his mind.

Andrews turned to the colonel. "I think the table is in almost unanimous agreement with your plan. We'll give these men," he nodded towards the civil servants, "the chance to consult with their Ministers, and then it's all systems go."

The residents along the Bayswater Road remained, for the large part, untouched by the evacuation plans. No incidents of note, since the death of Fred Dempsey's guard dog, had taken place there and the sector was the least well-guarded side of the square which the Army had cordoned off.

In his bedroom, Mark Dempsey slept fitfully after a massive sedative administered by the doctor. It had been almost three hours since his attack on his father and already the drug was beginning to wear off. The doctor had expressed amazement at the child's resistance to the injections and was due to return to the house within four hours to administer another dose if necessary.

Mark's body stirred under the thin cotton sheet, his head tossed from side to side and then, suddenly, he was awake, wide awake, senses quivering, his mind in turmoil. He began to cry out but stopped himself. The muted sound lay dead on the night air. The net curtains in his bedroom rustled in a soft, lapping motion, disturbed by a caressing current of warm air. The turmoil in his mind receded. He had been haunted in sleep by a bewildering series of images. His mind was now clear of them. He knew what he had to do.

The cotton sheet slipped softly from his body as he rose, naked, and stepped forward to the window. He gently reached out to touch the curtain, drawing aside the flimsy material to let the air wash over him. He shivered slightly as he stood there. The Bayswater Road lay dead before him. No cars drove on it. Across the road, the park slumbered under a moonless sky. Leaves whispered softly.

Mark plunged through the window, grasped the drainpipe and shinned down with graceful, noiseless speed.

He stood for a second, his head slightly cocked to one side, as if listening to a distant call.

"I'm coming," he whispered, running across the lawn, his feet skating over the soft grass. Within seconds he was racing along the hard concrete of the street. A drowsy soldier peered into the darkness, imagining that he had seen a body caught in the glare of a spotlight, but he dismissed the thought from his mind. He wasn't interested in humans tonight. The sky above the area glowed brightly with reflected light. Without a second thought the boy started climbing up the side of a nearby building. With incredibly sure footing he seemed to slide up the brickwork. Once on the flat roof he began running at breakneck speed as he plummeted over skylights, racing from building to building with leaping strides. His body, lathered in sweat, seemed to avoid obstacles instinctively. He ran, hunched over, his hands occasionally grazing against the ground in front.

Within a few minutes he had reached the end of the line of parallel roofs. He swung himself over the edge of the last building and began climbing downwards. When his feet touched the ground, he leaped around to find himself face to face with an astonished soldier. The young man held a rifle trained on the child.

"Here, you. Stop right there. Bloody lunatic." He stepped towards Mark. Suddenly his rifle had been wrenched from his grasp and he was lying in the gutter, blood seeping from his cracked skull.

The boy continued his journey, hugging the walls of the houses, darting into alleyways where they afforded protection, passing noiselessly within inches of soldiers looking the other way. When he came to a metal wire fence, he scaled it in a bound. He searched quickly around the waste-ground, conscious of the lights which illuminated his movements. Coming across a pile of rubble, he began to scramble amongst the debris until a small hole had appeared. He sat on his haunches for a moment, looking down into the darkness. "I'm coming," he whispered and was immediately swallowed up by the ground. He fell for some ten feet, landing easily on his feet and groped about in the total blackness. He scrambled at the earth for a few seconds, feeling it shift under his fingers. The tunnel was so narrow that he had to wriggle along on his stomach, roots and stones digging into his exposed flesh. He was getting closer, he could feel it. When the tunnel had come to an end, he stood bolt upright and hoisted himself upwards. He stood in the long, low underground room, searching for the exit. He could hear them clearly now. A door creaked open. He moved towards it, slipped through and rapidly climbed the stairs beyond. The purring noise grew in intensity as he ascended.

Crowther, Inglis, and the professor had begun to traverse the area by jeep again immediately after the conference. Jock Campbell had succumbed to the need for sleep. The streets of Paddington were like an immense film set, the buildings bare and harsh in the glare. The soldiers were still searching steadily, cautious and alert, their eyes screwed up tight in the violent lights.

"Some of these men look just like children," the professor remarked.

Something gelled in Crowther's mind. Children. "Inglis, what was the name of the boy that was looking after your cats."

"Mark. He's the son of that MP, Fred Dempsey. I'd forgotten all about him, I must admit."

"So had I." Crowther remembered the scene in the garden: the boy pushing him aside with extraordinary power, his hypnotized eyes, collapsing into the dead cats. It wasn't the kind of thing one remembered willingly. Within minutes, the three men were standing on Fred Dempsey's lawn explaining their mission to a policeman. He relented after Crowther showed his badge.

They were ushered into the splendidly decorated living room. It was almost five minutes before Fred Dempsey appeared in an elegant silk dressing gown. He was yawning and his hair was tousled. Crowther noted the heavy bandaging around one of his hands.

Dempsey stopped yawning when he saw Crowther. He recognized him as the rude young policeman from earlier in the day.

"Oh, it's you again. What the hell do you want now?"

"What happened to your hand?"

"None of your business. Who are these men?" Dempsey asked pointing at Inglis and the professor.

"That's not important. We've come in connection with the cats. We need to interview your son. It might prove very important."

The red flush crept up Dempsey's neck until it had suffused his whole face. "How damned preposterous. What's your superior's name? I'll phone him right away," Dempsey blurted out, moving threateningly towards the telephone.

Crowther walked up close to him, grabbed him by the lapels of his dressing gown and began speaking urgently.

"Listen to me, for God's sake. I've had enough of this big, important MP crap. I'm not interested in you or your damn influence. I am interested in the three hundred people lying dead in the morgue this evening on account of the cats. I need to see your son and I'm going to see him," his teeth clenched together in a grimace that frightened Dempsey, "even if I have to punch your stupid head in to do it. GET ME?"

Dempsey stood speechless for a moment. The policeman wasn't joking. He turned silently and walked up the stairs. He stopped at the top and, looking down, said, "I'll bring him down."

Crowther nervously paced the carpet. There was a cry from upstairs. Looking through the open door of the living room, Crowther could see Dempsey leaping down the stairs. "He's gone," he cried as he raced into the room. Crowther thundered up the stairs and into the empty bedroom. He flew to the window and stared out desperately but there was nothing.

Back in the living room he explained the boy's connection with the savage events of the day. Dempsey, his face white with shock, admitted that his son had attacked him earlier in the evening. He untraveled the bandages on his hand to let them see the terrible wound.

"Mr. Dempsey," the professor began, after examining the MP's bloody scar, "I realize how dreadfully upsetting this all is, but I must ask you one question. Does your son suffer from any of these diseases?" He withdrew a slip of paper from his pocket and handed it to Dempsey, who, blinking tears of panic from his eyes, accepted it and began to read. He was about halfway down when a sharp intake of breath told the professor all he wanted to know.

"Which one, man?"

Dempsey held the paper out with a trembling hand and pointed at it with his index finger. "This one. The kidney disease. Had it all his life. Born with it. I was about to take him to the hospital for dialysis in the morning. For God's sake, tell me what it means!"

"It means, Mr. Dempsey," said Vole, having taken a deep breath and having decided to tell him the truth, "that your son is suffering from a disease that has affected his brain cells. In effect, he is suffering from the same disease as the cats."

Dempsey began to shake, first his shoulders and then his whole body. Crowther stepped forward just in time to stop him from falling onto the floor.

CHAPTER FOURTEEN

Crowther woke with a start, stared briefly around the room at the other sleeping figures hunched uncomfortably on camp beds, and knew immediately that this day was somehow different from its predecessor. He glanced at his watch. Half past seven. Someone should have woken them an hour before. He walked to the window and stared out over Paddington. The scene below was much as he had expected. Military reinforcements had been arriving during the night and there was hardly a spot of daylight between the massed ranks of soldiers that encircled the area. The TV cameras and radio reporters were out in force, clumped together in ragged groups just beyond the waiting lines. Behind them were rows of ambulances and fire engines. Everything as expected, and yet something was wrong.

It took Crowther a full minute to realize what it was. The sun was hidden by a dense layer of cloud and a light drizzle dripped from the sky. All the civilians on the ground were wearing raincoats. The weather had turned.

Crowther reached forward to unlatch the window and breathed in the air. Pure and fresh and distinctly cold. A slight breeze ruffled his hair and he combed it quickly before turning to wake his companions.

"Wake up, gentlemen, I've got a surprise for you."

John Inglis, his hair a wild mass of entangled curls, leapt, Medusa-like, from his pillow, his eyes wide open, his body shivering as if he had been disturbed in the middle of an unsettling dream. The professor came awake by stages, grunting and mumbling and smacking his lips. With a reflex motion, his eyes still shut, he began unbuttoning his shirt, mistaking it for a pajama top.

Crowther grinned. "I wouldn't bother, Professor. You'll just have to put it on again. Come over to the window." The two men stumbled from their makeshift beds and craned their heads out into the air.

Vole brought his head in sharply, like a tortoise.

"Extremely cold, I must say. Pity the poor soldiers who've been standing out there all night."

Inglis pulled the window shut when he had finished scanning the streets below and stood for a moment, lost in thought.

"You know what this means?" he asked.

Crowther nodded. "A brief respite, at least. Let's go and see what's happening."

Vole stretched out his hand to restrain the young man's impatience. "I have great admiration for your enthusiasm, Sergeant, but I have learnt from long years of experience that hard days are best started on bulging stomachs. Kindly lead us to your canteen. I need at least seven cups of tea before my mind starts functioning."

Crowther laughed. "Professor, it'll be a bloody miracle if your mind functions at all after our canteen food."

They had eaten heartily, in silence for the most part, before going in a group to the Chief Inspector's office. Andrews looked at them with a faint air of guilt as they filed into the room.

"Good morning to you all and how are you feeling? Good. Now, as you no doubt know, it's raining cats and d …" He blushed. "Hardly an appropriate metaphor given the context. It's raining outside and it's fairly nippy. If your theory holds good, Professor, and the Ministry of Defence suggest that it will, the cats won't attack for the moment."

"Has anything turned up in the last couple of hours?" Crowther asked.

"Nothing. God knows where they've gone. However, we do have one important development. While searching in the basement office belonging to the WLBC radio station, soldiers discovered two bodies."

"So what?" asked Inglis. "There's plenty more in the morgue."

"Yes, but this was a bit different. Apparently they had suffocated to death. There were no marks on them at all, and the wall on one side of the room had caved in. When they had cleared away the rubble, the troops discovered a tunnel."

There was a sharp intake of breath from the listeners. "Exactly. They followed it for a while, some two hundred yards and they came across some cats who must have been crushed to death. The two men must have been standing in the room when the wall collapsed. The cats must have made the wall collapse, crushing the men, but, judging by the lack of visible wounds, the animals didn't attack them. That means it happened after the temperature had cooled, and after the cats had gone to ground. Their deaths were probably accidental, poor blighters."

"What about the tunnel?" Vole asked breathlessly.

"It must have caved in during the night. The soldiers said they could hear it collapsing ahead of them, so it might even have happened while they were searching it. We've got all kinds of digging equipment down there now. Once we've found where it leads, we'll have gone some way to solving our problem."

"That's marvelous," the professor enthused. "Wonderful."

"Yes it is," Andrews agreed, "but we have another little problem."

"What's that?" the three men chorused.

"The Home Secretary and the Minister of Defence are intending to pay us a visit here in about half an hour."

Inglis looked at the Inspector suspiciously. "What's so bad about that? They should give us everything we want."

Andrews shook his head sadly. "Quite the opposite, I'm afraid."

The people grouped around the troubled streets of Paddington began to wonder if God had not decided to intervene in the unholy affair. In the worsening rain the hysteria of the previous day rapidly became a dim memory and the screaming banner headlines of the early-morning editions of Fleet Street newspapers began to take on an almost historical air. The crowds, who had been gathering since dawn, quickly became bored by the lack of action and began to break up, wandering back to their offices or homes. If anything happened, they consoled themselves, they could pick it up on the television. The troops shivered uncomfortably in the annoying rain as the dampness of their uniforms began to seep through to their tired, aching limbs. Officers patrolled the lines constantly in an attempt to cheer up their men. The reporters lounged disconsolately around the TV equipment trucks, some playing cards, others just watching the grey clouds. Perhaps it had just been the weather driving the cats mad. It happened to people sometimes, so why not animals? Had they really all got so excited over a bunch of lousy cats? It hardly seemed feasible. The troops, the reporters, the ambulance men and the firefighters stared at the sky and prayed that the rain would end soon and that the sun would come out to warm them.

"Are you being serious?" Vole thundered, banging his fist in frustration on the conference room table. "Have you gone bloody mad, man?"

The Home Secretary looked stonily down the table at him. "Professor, I never joke about serious situations and I am most certainly not a lunatic. This is my decision and I have made it. The troops are to be pulled back and the people of this area allowed back into their homes. I think you have all totally overestimated the gravity of events. The population of London is in a state of total panic. There have been reports of drunken mobs out patrolling the streets killing every stray cat they find from here to Watford Gap. I feel the social consequences of your actions here far outweigh considerations of safety."

Inglis raised his hand for attention. The Home Secretary nodded for him to speak. "Thank you, sir. You're a liar." A gasp went up around the table. "There are thousands of people outside who've turned up to see the cats. If they were in a state of panic, as you suggest, they'd be doing everything in their power to get out of town, and damned fast. And I can't believe you're asking us to worry about a few cats getting bumped off in the rest of London. Too damned many of them anyway, as those poor sods who died yesterday would no doubt testify if they had a chance."

The Home Secretary started to speak but Crowther, taking his life in his hands, interrupted him. Andrews shot him a dirty look, but he carried on. "Could I just ask, sir, if the Minister of Defence shares your views?"

The Minister in question leant forward, made as if to speak, changed his mind and nodded resolutely instead.

The Home Secretary continued. "Gentlemen, I don't intend to put up with any more of this. My decision is final. You have shown me no proof that the animals will break out again. In fact, you can't even tell me where they are. I don't believe they're cowering below ground waiting for the right moment to strike again. The whole thing's preposterous. If the truth be told, they're probably just dispersed into their owner's houses or wherever they came from in the first place. You're all acting like hysterical children."

"Home Secretary," the professor rose from his seat. "You are a damned scoundrel. The reason you want this hushed up is that your tottering government wouldn't survive the scandal of it allowing the details of a dangerous official chemical weapons experiment to fall into the hands of someone who was able to replicate it in a bloody London basement! National elections are due to take place in two weeks and that's the real reason you're willing to risk the lives of thousands of innocent people. Just to ensure re-election. I shall personally make it my business to tell the public what you did here. Not that I'll probably have to. When a few thousand more people have died, perhaps the British populace will see you for the cheap, twisting charlatan you really are."

The Home Secretary rose to his feet with a bellow of rage that had been growing inside him during Vole's speech but found himself competing with the shrill sound of a ringing telephone. Crowther reached behind him and picked the offending instrument up, listened for a few moments and turned, with a look of triumph, to the Home Secretary. "I'm afraid we won't have much time to implement your instructions, sir. A group of cats have been sighted in the streets." The Home Secretary collapsed back into his chair as if he had just been hit full in the stomach.

Mikey tipped his head back and allowed the last remnants of a bottle of beer to trickle down into his open throat. When he had drained it, he let out a gasp of satisfaction and with a swinging motion of his arm threw the bottle through the ornate pub window. He'd always wanted to do that. With raucous whoops of approval, his six companions took up his lead and began breaking every piece of glass in the tavern. Mikey grinned at them for a while, passing disparaging remarks about the accuracy of their aim and their relative weakness. Mikey was two years older than most of them and they treated him like God. He was sixteen years old and already on the dole queue. He had given up looking for work after a few months. There had seemed so little point. The work that was available to him seemed so dull and he could just about eke out a living on unemployment payments and the occasional bit of thieving. It wasn't a bad life, he reflected, opening another bottle. He guzzled for a few seconds, then a strange sound caught his attention.

He silenced his companions with a signal and listened carefully. There it was again. A human voice. He gazed around the room, his small, pig-like eyes darting from side to side.

There was a cupboard underneath the stairs leading up to the living quarters attached to the inn. Mikey walked towards it and bent his head to the wood to listen. The sobs were fading away but were quite distinct. He kicked at the door. There was a loud shriek.

"All right, open up, or I'll kick it in." His followers gathered around him as the door creaked, moved a tentative inch and then swung open. Mikey bent down and dragged the girl out and stood back to look at her.

She was no more than seventeen years of age, but tall and attractive in an odd way. Her flimsy summer dress clung tightly to her shapely body. Wide, frightened brown eyes gazed out at Mikey from behind the strands of long blonde hair that were plastered over her face.

She sniffled nervously and the streaks of dirt on her cheeks

showed that she had been crying. Her lower lip hung, pendu-
lous and trembling, giving her an air of simplemindedness that
proved to be correct when Mikey began questioning her.

"Who are you?" She remained silent. "What were you doing
in there, eh?"

"Frightened… I was frightened."

"Who by?"

"Cats … they came … hid," she jabbed a grimy finger
towards the gaping door of the cupboard. "Hid."

"You stupid or somethin', bitch?" The girl made no reply,
but raised one of her hands to her face and began playing with
her lower lip, like a confused child.

Mikey laughed harshly. "Yeah, well, you might be stupid,
but you don't half look good, darling." He laughed again and
moved menacingly towards her. She shifted uneasily, her feet
inching backwards and dived for the cupboard. Mikey had her
in his grasp immediately, pulling her roughly to the ground.
His friends began shouting excitedly, egging him on. With one
rip her dress was off. He sank his mouth greedily onto her ripe,
cherry-like nipples and began sucking frantically as his hands
grasped at her tights. She was screaming and one of her flailing hands caught Mikey's cheek. He stopped struggling for a
moment and reached up to touch his skin. When he brought
his hand away, there was blood on it from the ugly wound her
nails had inflicted. He slapped her hard across the face and she
lay back, momentarily stunned. "You dirty whore, I'm gonna
make you pay for that. Yeah, me and all my mates." He sank on
top of her, forcing her legs apart with his thrusting knee. "Yeah,
darlin', bet you never had it like this, eh?" he croaked, his voice
husky with lust.

He looked up quickly. The room was silent. His companions were staring towards the pub door, their faces dumb with
amazement. Mikey struggled to his feet.

The naked boy stood framed in the doorway. Mikey
approached him cautiously. "Who the bleedin' hell are you?"
The boy made no answer. "Here, I'm talking to you. Cat got
your tongue?" His friends brayed with laughter. Mikey took
a few steps towards him, but stopped. There was something

about the boy's gaze, the way he held his eyes without a flicker of fear, that made him feel uneasy. He had to act quickly before the others saw his nervousness. As he stood there, a thought came to him. There had been something he had always wanted to do, and this was the ideal opportunity. His whole life had been bound up with violence, from the school playground to the football terraces and Saturday night dances. He had punched, kicked, gouged and stabbed many times, but he had never killed. He had seen it done. Once, in the alleyway behind the old West London terraced house in which he had lived as a child, he had seen a "grass", a police informant, caught by some local gangsters. He had been six years old, playing with a spinning top. The killing had been done with razors, the cut-throat variety, that had sliced with deceptive ease deep into the flesh of the screaming, terrified victim. The scene had left the youngster flushed and excited and he had often dreamt about it. He could feel the sensation returning as he stood watching the naked boy.

This was the perfect chance to try a killing. There was no one around except his mates and they were too frightened of him to go to the police. News of the deed might even get into the right ears. The local gangsters might even notice him, offer him a job, and once you worked for them, nobody bothered you. Not even the cops.

His companions were now quiet and staring expectantly at their leader. He turned to them slowly, savoring the dramatic effect. "All right, boys, watch this. This is the big one. I'm going to kill this little bastard." There was a yelp from the girl behind him. "Don't worry, darling, your turn will come." One of the boys began to protest but Mikey silenced him with a sharp glance.

He bent down and picked up a broken Guinness bottle that nestled against his feet. He gripped the neck lovingly and turned the glinting, jagged end towards the naked child. The intruder remained still.

"Okay, boys, leave it to Mikey. You can have him when I've finished." There was a scrambling noise behind him. He turned just as the girl was about to pounce on him. With two swift movements he tripped her up and kicked her squarely in the face as she fell to the ground. He watched her as she lay there groaning for a second and turned back to the doorway.

With measured steps he advanced on his quarry.

"NO!" the boy's shout was so loud that Mikey almost dropped his bottle.

Then the boy said, "Come, friends," in a quiet voice. The cats poured through the doorway silently and stood protectively round the boy's legs. With shouts of fear, Mikey's companions turned to escape but found themselves faced with another line of cats who had slipped in through the broken windows on the other side of the bar.

Mikey lunged desperately forward, the gaping jaws of the bottle aimed at the child's face. The boy sidestepped, hand-chopped the broken bottle out of his assailant's hand and, with a snarl of pure hatred, sank his teeth deep into Mikey's exposed neck.

CHAPTER FIFTEEN

It was 10 AM exactly when the conference room was informed of the reappearance of the cats near the southern sector of the area. By that time, the refugees temporarily housed in the giant tents that had engulfed Hyde Park during the night had begun to file out into the welcome sunlight despite the attempts of the soldiers on guard to keep them inside. They had sat all morning inside the vast canvas domes, morose and petulant, grumbling about the food they were offered. But, with the coming of the sun, the general pall of depression swiftly lifted. They emerged from the tents in a sudden rush, breathing in the air, laughing in the warming sunlight.

Sporadic games of football broke out as clusters of children started kicking empty Coca Cola cans around. The adults, after stretching their legs a bit, lay down on the damp grass. A few packs of cards were produced and, within minutes, a number of gambling schools had been set up. The soldiers walked cheerfully amongst their charges, pleased not to be facing anger or resentment

In the distance, through the lush foliage of the trees that ran along the Bayswater Road, the people could just make out the tall, white houses that marked the entrance to Lancaster Gate, the up-market end of Paddington. A few of them even set off determinedly with the avowed intention of returning to their homes, but were hastily turned back by the troops. All in all they took it good-naturedly. In a few swift minutes, the memories of the day before receded to be replaced by skepticism and good humor.

The helicopters weaved back and forth through the sky, the

pilots marveling at the sight of seventy thousand people enjoying the sun. They spotted the animals at the same time as the toddler.

Through the delighted yells of the playing children could be discerned a more strident human noise. On the outskirts of the crowd, a young child sat, gurgling contentedly, its fat, stubby arms jabbing forwards. It squealed with pleasure. The child's father bent down and tousled its filmy golden locks and then glanced in the direction its hands were pointing.

Soldiers were streaming across the grass towards them, evidently panicked. To aid their escape, they had dropped their weapons. A few tripped and, with the jerking, spastic motions of desperation, got to their feet again to maintain their flight.

The child's father stood up slowly, a terrible suspicion gripping his heart. A few more of the crowd had got up to watch the curious behavior of the soldiers.

Within seconds their worst fears had been confirmed. As if it had received one mighty electric shock, the rest of the crowd rose to its feet, all conversation silenced. Some forty yards behind the troops, emerging from under the low-hung branches of the trees, came the cats skating over the wet grass like a giant, living puck on an ice-hockey rink. The crowd began to edge backwards, carefully at first, but when they saw what the animals did to the soldiers they caught, they turned, arms flailing, legs trampling, clambering over each other to get away. Many found themselves crushed up against the sides of the tents, which swayed and tottered dangerously under the onslaught. A large part of the crowd, some with children clasped in their arms, made for the entrances to the tents and rushed inside, while others kept heading across the park towards Knightsbridge and Park Lane.

A few army jeeps bounced madly across the grass to interpose themselves between the animals and the fleeing population, but a couple of bursts of machine-gun fire were all they managed before being overwhelmed by a tide of cats.

Once they were through the puny defenses the animals made straight for the tents, into which people were still pouring. The cats made short work of the stragglers and reached

the entrances within seconds before flooding through the narrow canvas flaps. For almost two minutes dreadful shrieking
sounds filled the air. The tents billowed and sagged as people
threw themselves against the sides trying to escape. One or two
managed to crawl out through the front, but were soon caught
and killed. Others attempted to squeeze underneath the sides
of the tightly-secured tents, but only got caught halfway, their
eyes bulging with pain as the animals inside began to eat into
their spines.

Outside, the helicopters hovered, powerless to act. From
all directions the troops began to move in, guns ready, their
long spell of boredom thankfully ended. As they approached
the tents, a light film of drizzle began to pour out of the sky,
sheeting gently down, shimmering in the continuing sun. A
faint rainbow illuminated the horizon. Within seconds, the cats
had begun to pour out of the canvas domes and were racing
back over the grass towards the section of the Bayswater Road
from which they had appeared. The troops were not far enough
advanced to make an attack on them, but the animals' progress
was halted by helicopters that swooped in low on top of them,
jets of flame spurting from flamethrowers held by precariously
perched co-pilots. Seven helicopters in all had converged on
the escaping mass, each taking it in turns to fall to about five
yards from the ground before ascending, its work done. One
co-pilot, leaning too far from his 'copter, fell from the side door
at the lowest point of the dive. He bounced to his feet as soon
as he hit the ground, scattering the animals around him, the
flamethrower still miraculously in his hands. Yelling with fear
and excitement, he blasted fountains of flame into the ground
around him, scorching the grass for several yards and frying
animals until he was surrounded by a neat pile of charred car-
casses. He waited until the last of the cats had passed him and
then he turned, running after them, his machine belching fire.
When they had got out of range, the co-pilot collapsed, sobbing
and laughing in turns, to the ground.

"All right, shut up!" Andrews shouted to get some order. A
free-for-all argument had ensued after the news of the attack

in the park, each contingent blaming the other for the inadequate forces on the southern side of the danger area, and for the Army's inability to destroy the cats on their return journey.

"Now," Andrews continued. "Let's look at this sensibly. They've had the upper hand from the very start. Let's just make sure that our next engagement with the enemy is decisive. Let's look at the situation and ask some relevant questions. Have any of the animals escaped into other parts of London? We can't really tell, but our helicopter pilots seem fairly sure that they haven't, so we still have them boxed up in this area." He pointed vaguely at the map behind him. "And that's the most important thing of all. Once they get outside of that square, that's it. We'll never get them under control. Now, we do hold another trump card that none of you know about. A few minutes ago a message came through that we have located the lair of the cats."

Andrews smiled as a gasp went up around the table. "In view of that fact, I have drawn up a little plan that might meet with general approval." He smiled knowingly.

Duke Inglis had been standing behind the troops from first light, waiting for an opportunity to slip through the cordon. He had had a lot of time to reflect during the night. With the aid of jet lag he had not slept a wink and had spent the time thinking about his son. He had decided that, if the boy was alive, he would stop hounding him. There was so little point. Just once before he died, though, he would like to tell John why he thought things had gone so wrong between them. For that he needed to get into the Westbourne Terrace apartment.

In the initial confusion following the news of the attack in the park, Inglis slipped through the line of troops and marched resolutely across the road. He had memorized a map of the area on the preceding night and began to slip through the side streets with some assurance, calculating precisely where his son's flat would be.

He descended the steps quickly. The room was dark and he smoothed his hand against the cool, plastered wall until he found the light switch. The strip lights flickered for a few moments and the laboratory was bathed in a harsh, unnatural glow. Inglis picked his way between the two rows of cages and plonked himself into the desk seat. He looked around him, recognizing his son's spidery handwriting on the bottles and test tubes above his head.

He began to sift through the desk drawers, pulling out letters, postcards and bills addressed to John Glissin. Amongst this new batch of correspondence were some older, crumpled letters which had been sent by the senator himself, addressed to the university. At least the boy had cared enough to keep them, he reflected. After he had finished with the drawers he began leafing through the material arranged over the desk top. Mostly they were notebooks with chemical symbols and incomprehensible diagrams. At the bottom of the pile was a large, blue notebook with "TESTS-REPORTS" printed on the cover in large capital letters. Inglis opened it and leafed through the pages for several minutes. When he had finished, he closed it slowly, put it back carefully on the desk and cursed. So his son had been responsible for the mayhem outside. If the boy was still alive, perhaps he would really need to get out of the country. Well, the senator could arrange that with no trouble at all.

Inglis sighed, reached into his pocket for a pen, found a clean sheet of paper and began to write. He would leave a note for John in which he would try to explain his change of heart, his deep need to have him back by his side and his sorrow for the past. He would also offer to help him out of his present predicament. Finally, he would have to leave an address where he could be contacted. He would give John a week. By then he would know if the boy was dead or simply didn't wish to see him. He prayed fervently that the latter reason would turn out to be the real one.

For a man whose life had been spent using the tortuous language of politics, the expression of his innermost feelings was no easy thing, and the senator had to stop often to search his mind for a phrase that would be accurate and would sound sincere. When he had finished there were tears in his eyes. He folded the sheet of paper, wrote his son's name on the outside, and placed it in the center of the desk where it would be quickly spotted.

He sat back in his chair and closed his eyes, drained emotionally by the effort of composition. His mind went blank for a few moments and he almost fell asleep. Something pulled him back to full consciousness. Sounds. Scuffling sounds. He opened his eyes. He was staring upwards through the basement window and could see rows and rows of cats slinking down the street. His mind went back to the previous day's newscasts. He decided to lock himself in the flat and turn off the lights. It might be his only chance.

He had an uneasy feeling as he walked down the corridor between the cages. He looked up quickly. Through the basement window some six feet above his head, a cat was peering malevolently down at him. He started to run towards the door, but was stopped short about halfway there. There had been a soft but distinct mewing sound that froze him in his tracks. Out of the corner of his eye he saw a movement. From the cage nearest to him on his left-hand side, a cat's head slowly protruded. The animal surveyed him dispassionately. Instinctively the senator began to move backwards, the cat still staring at him. Before he had gone two feet, his heels bumped against an object. He craned his neck to look behind him. The animals were arranged at short intervals along the floor all the way back to the desk. When he looked back towards the door, they had arranged themselves in a similar fashion in front of him. His escape route was completely blocked.

They must have been waiting in the cages, biding their time until he made a move—a move that brought him out of the reach of any weapons. He had to think quickly, more quickly than ever before. He had been in tough situations during the war, but none as tough as this. Suppressing the shivers of apprehension that had begun to shake his body, he lunged for the nearest cage, lifted it high above his head and plunged it in front of him down the corridor, scattering the animals lying in wait for him, and took to his heels. He knew his chances outside were slim, but inside the laboratory they were non-existent. He had almost reached the door when two blurred shapes flew through the air from the cages on either side of him. He felt a sharp, stabbing pain in his cheek and the revolting sensation of small, jagged teeth gripping his throat. With extraordinary agility he pivoted on his feet and ran for the far wall, smashing straight into it. The animal at his throat, stunned, loosened its grip and thudded to the floor. With a loud shout of triumph, the senator opened the door of the flat and stepped out into the corridor.

They were waiting for him. The stairs leading directly up the front door of the building were covered by cats. He recognized, about eight steps up, the animal that had been staring down at him from the street. He turned swiftly just as they began to move towards him, leapt back into the laboratory and locked the door. There were about fifteen cats left in the narrow room. The senator leant his back against the door for a moment, sobbing for breath and then he smiled.

"Okay, you little bastards, come and get me!"

They moved with great deliberation, never taking their eyes off him until they were ranged in two lines across his path. The senator watched the regrouping with keen interest.

He laughed loudly. "So, that's your game. Well, you got me. I'm a cornered man and there's only one thing I can do." His skin glistened with sweat. He unbuttoned his coat with deliberate care and held it in front of him. Behind he could hear the sound of paws scraping against the wooden door, getting more insistent by the second. Then came the thuds as the cats began to hurl themselves against the entrance to the lab. Finally he heard the wood begin to splinter.

With a scream of pure aggression he leapt forward, throwing his wide coat over the waiting foe. He leapt clear over the two lines of animals and raced back down towards the desk, pulling the cages down by either side of him as he ran. Each cage brought a fresh scream as one of the pursuing cats got caught by its fall.

By the time he had reached the desk, one of the animals had attached itself to his back and another was hanging onto his leg, its teeth biting straight through his trousers and into the skin. He swirled round and crashed his back against the rows of test tubes and bottles. The cat on his back was crushed in an instant. It gave a hoarse gasp as the air gushed from its lungs. He stooped to pick up the heavy desk chair and brought it swinging down on his leg, stunning his other attacker. Reaching behind him, he grasped a bottle full of chemicals and rammed it down onto the cat's skull.

As he looked up, the door to the laboratory cracked open and swung loose on its hinges.

"Come on, boys," he screamed. "There's plenty for all of ya. I'm taking some of you sons of bitches with me."

As they began to advance, he turned to the rows of bottles, found the one he wanted, and removed it from the shelf. He swung around to find the ringleader looking at him from no more than five yards. The cat was entirely black, larger than the rest, and the group stayed slightly behind him.

"You," the senator shouted. "You're the bastard I want. I've got something for you." He carefully took the stopper out of the bottle. Faint wisps of smoke rose upwards from it. The black cat pounced into the air, straight for the big man. The senator's huge hand lashed out, clasped the animal by the throat and pinned it against the wall. Its jaws gaped open in rage and frustration. With his other hand, the senator took the open bottle and thrust it sharply down the cat's throat, upending the acid straight down its gullet. He chuckled as the animal wailed and stared straight into its hate-filled eyes. The senator let it drop and watched it crawl in agony for a few moments on the ground. With a sadistic cackle he brought his foot crashing down on its head.

He swung round just in time to fend off the first attack by the black cat's guards. He reached out to the shelf and got down two more bottles of sulphuric acid. He had the tops off in a second. With one grasped securely in each hand, he advanced up the corridor, flailing the liquid from side to side like a priest dispensing Holy Water. The animals began to scramble out of his path, terrified of the stinging fluid. The huge man snarled and kicked at them as his triumphal procession continued. When he had reached the open door, he spun round and threw the two bottles back up the corridor and grinned in satisfaction at the fresh screams of pain. The joy of victory coursed through him as he started to ascend the stairs.

The senator was so preoccupied that he did not see the cat

until it was too late. It was massive, even larger than the brother he had just killed. He saw the black shape at the last moment. It smashed into his chest, sending Inglis reeling back down the stairs. His head crashed on the bottom rung and he was stunned. He opened his eyes at the last moment to see the gaping jaws descending on his throat. The animal's teeth made a neat incision in the senator's jugular vein and dark, red blood began to pump in violent, rhythmic spurts from his body. "You can't win 'em all," he croaked as the life began to ebb from him.

CHAPTER SIXTEEN

"Okay, let's go," Jock Campbell said, pulling on his jacket. "No, wait a minute," Crowther answered and pushed the rewind button on the small portable tape recorder.

Campbell gave an exasperated sigh. "Look, laddy, I'm your boss, and don't forget it. The cats have been sighted again on the streets, the temperature's past seventy-four degrees, and I don't want to miss the action. We're going to fix the little buggers this time."

Campbell, Inglis and Vole stood impatiently by the door as Crowther got to the part of the tape he wanted and turned up the volume.

"Delta 70 calling. The cats are racing back towards Paddington. We're just about to make our dive. The fire seems to be having an effect. We're diving … now. Hang on. Good God. I can't be sure, but I thought I just saw … it can't be. Yes, there it is again. It looks like there's a kid down there. He's naked. He's pretty young and he's running with the cats, bent right forward on all fours. It's ridiculous, but he's there. Am I going nuts?"

Crowther switched the machine off and turned back to the group by the door.

"Well, now we know where Mark Dempsey is. How the hell are we going to tell his old man?"

"God knows," said Campbell. "Let's worry about that later. Perhaps we can save the kid."

The professor shook his head. "I'm afraid he's gone for good. There's no way of reversing the process. I wish there were."

The men were silent for a moment before turning towards the door.

The troops were alert and eager for action. Their superiors had erred badly with the incident in the Park. Over seven hundred people had been killed in the lightning attack and everyone was blaming the Army, firstly for not having the southern section of the cordon as closely guarded as the rest, and secondly for allowing the animals back into the area when the slaughter had finished. The fact that many of them had been killed made no difference. Every time they attacked there seemed to be more of them. It had just dawned on the military that only a part of the entire force was sent on each mission, like a conventional army. The thought of meeting them all at once was not generally relished. Anyway, the troops felt that, in some odd way, the shame of their officers devolved on them. They were determined not to let another opportunity go by.

News of the attack in the Park had brought the crowds back in force, larger than ever, and they stood massed behind the troops, shouting insults to raucous accompanying laughter. The soldiers gritted their teeth and tried to take it in good humor. Their superiors had worked out a plan and it was a good one. When sufficiently large numbers of the cats had been reported above ground, the troops would move in from the east, driving the animals back towards the stationary western cordon which would remain firmly in position, come what may. With the cats safely sandwiched between the lines of troops, they would be destroyed by fire. It was a prospect the soldiers enjoyed. Many of them had seen their companions killed, or watched their torn bodies being carried from Hyde Park. It tinged all their actions with the all-powerful desire for revenge.

Despite requests that he keep at home, Fred Dempsey was waiting for them by the Army jeeps. Crowther walked over to him. "I thought we told you to stay away. There's nothing you can usefully do here and, anyway, think of the publicity."

The MP gave a wry smile. "Perhaps it's time I stopped caring about politics and my career and started thinking about human beings instead." Crowther, unable to think of a suitable reply, ushered him into the nearest jeep.

Inglis, who was standing nearby, looked at Dempsey strangely for a moment. Would his own father ever come around to the same point of view, or was that too much to hope for? It was no wonder to him that he had got on so well with young Mark Dempsey. Their backgrounds were remarkably similar.

A tap on his arm broke through his thoughts. A uniformed policeman was standing by his side.

"Excuse me, sir, are you Mr. Inglis?"

"That's correct."

"I thought I'd better tell you that, while I was on duty at the Park Gate yesterday, a gentleman approached me and asked about a John Inglis resident in Westbourne Terrace. I remember the incident because he was most insistent and I had to check through the whole list of refugees."

John steeled himself to ask the next question. "What did he look like?"

"Very striking," the policeman replied. "Tall gentleman, white hair, very burly. About six four, fifteen stone. American, like yourself."

Inglis felt a sinking sensation in his stomach. There could be no doubt about it. His father had caught up with him at last, and what a moment for it to happen. "Thank you, Constable," he muttered abstractedly. The copper nodded and moved away. His mind still thoroughly preoccupied, Inglis got into the jeep with Crowther, Dempsey and Professor Vole.

Soldiers stretched away on either side of them as far as they could see. Jeeps were stationed at fifteen yard intervals along the line, most with machine guns and flamethrowers attached to the front. The eastern line was ready to move, none more so than Jock Campbell who had somehow placed himself in charge of the jeeps. He was in the vehicle three along from Crowther, parked slightly in front of the others. Crowther caught sight of him pulling on a hipflask. Crowther didn't have to guess what it contained. He smiled to himself. It felt good to have the old man so near at such a dangerous time.

Jock Campbell put away the flask, wiped a dribble of whisky from his chin and gave a merry wave. Crowther waved back. Behind him Inglis reached into the pocket of his denim coat and pulled out a glass bottle, removed a pill and swallowed it.

"Not illegal, I hope," asked Crowther slyly.

"No. Tranquillizers. Valium. I've been living on them for the last twenty-four hours." He replaced the bottle and sat staring at the instrument panel. Two thoughts were raging through his mind. How would he react if he saw the cats coming for him in a big bunch? Would he panic and run, or would it bring out the best fighting American spirit in him? At the same time he could not help thinking about his father. Where was the crazy old bastard? What would Inglis's reaction be if they met up? True, he still hated the old man. That was only natural, but would he be able to find it in his heart to forgive him? Inglis decided that he would at least try to make an effort. After all, if he was going to become his country's next president, someone had to rehabilitate the old rogue.

Vole sat in the back seat, his white, mottled teeth clamped firmly around the stem of his white, mottled pipe. He kept glancing nervously at his companion, Fred Dempsey, who seemed to be in a state of shellshock. The politician was staring into the middle distance, struggling with his conscience.

Vole decided to leave him alone in his silence and turned his attention to the road in front. The sun glinted brilliantly off the wet roads as the soldiers eagerly scanned them for a sight of the animals.

A shout from a specially-posted lookout on a rooftop behind them gave the alert. The men strained their eyes and within seconds what had previously seemed a trick of the light became a mass of distinctly moving bodies. The individual groups of cats scattered erratically about the area had merged into one main army and were advancing on the eastern cordon. It was heartening news for the Army commanders, since everything was falling into place according to their original plans.

The animals were about 180 yards down the broad tree-lined terrace, moving with their usual slow deliberation. Each muscle and sinew of the soldiers tightened imperceptibly with every advancing step. The crowd behind the military began to edge backwards. They hadn't expected their vigil to be quite so quickly rewarded.

Crowther heard an order bawled from somewhere to the right of him along the line which made no verbal sense. The troops rustled into full attention. Another shout followed seconds later and with a pounce they were off, the whole line of soldiers moving so fast up the avenue that the jeeps were almost caught by surprise. Crowther found himself having to motor quite fast to keep up with them and avoid the line of policemen bringing up the rear from running into his vehicle.

The Army had very definitely decided to change its tactics. The cats had already shown an uncanny knack for learning from previous encounters and were no doubt ready for solid defense on the part of the soldiers. Now the decision had been taken to attack as quickly and brutally as possible, thereby allowing the animals no time to devise an alternative escape route, and forcing them back towards the western cordon. There, the top military brass had a plan in place that—if successful—could quell the immediate menace, and restore the army's tarnished reputation at the same time. But first they had to drive the cats westwards.

At first the attack met with great success. It took the troops no more than thirty seconds to reach within twenty yards of the cats who, taken completely by surprise, stood still while the flamethrowers ranged destructively over their front line. Soon the soldiers were marching over charred bodies. Ahead of them, the cats began to move steadily backwards with all the precision of a military detachment. Calmly the cats back-stepped, managing to keep just out of the range of the flamethrowers, no matter how fast the troops advanced.

Soon the jeeps were bouncing over the dead animals, lurching from side to side, the wheels sometimes failing to get a proper grip on the squelching bodies.

"There he is!" Fred Dempsey jumped to his feet in the back of the vehicle, almost falling out, his hands stabbing excitedly ahead. Crowther followed the direction of his pointing finger. In the middle of the retreating group was a small clearing and every now and then could be glimpsed the white flesh of a human being. Clustered around him were four cats, all black, much larger than their colleagues, acting as bodyguards. It was

Mark Dempsey. Of that there could be no question. The MP made as if to jump from the moving car. The professor dived at him just as he was about to leap and brought him tumbling back into the back seat, where he held him fast. Dempsey struggled furiously, but the old man had a tenacious grip. The boy, who had been running on all fours, reared up momentarily and stared at them before crouching back on the ground. "Mark! Mark!" Dempsey yelled, his voice a hoarse scream of chilling desperation.

CHAPTER SEVENTEEN

Crowther placed his foot hard on the accelerator, but a series of shouts from behind caused him to stop the jeep.

They had been fooled. Pouring from every door and alleyway were hundreds of cats who had hidden themselves in preparation for the attack. They had waited until the main mass of troops had passed before showing themselves. Now, as they appeared, they divided themselves into two groups; one heading for the line of police advancing just behind the jeeps, the other heading for the laughably weak cordon of troops that had been left behind to guard the eastern section of the cordon. Crowther cried out in horror. There seemed no way that the soldiers remaining at the end of the avenue could stop the animals swarming past them into the crowded West End of London.

The police who had turned around to face the rearguard attack were in dreadful trouble and were near to being overwhelmed. Bravely they held their positions, firing randomly into the advancing mob. Their commander had been brought down immediately and they seemed to have little idea what to do.

"Fall back, fall back!" Jock Campbell bellowed, standing up in the driving seat of his jeep.

The policemen were not slow to obey. In some confusion they began to edge away from the continuous attack. Through the blue lines, Crowther could see the second wave of animals rapidly approaching the end of the terrace.

"Now, RUN!" The coppers turned and belted for it. As they began to clear the line of jeeps, Campbell reached into his back seat and brought out a flamethrower. The men in the other jeeps swiftly followed his example, and soon great sheets of white-hot flame spurted from the back of each vehicle. Crowther stepped forward into the back seat, standing between the professor and Dempsey and, with a rush of exhilaration, pulled the trigger on the American-made weapon and gave the animals one long, continuous blast. It felt good to be fighting them at last.

There was something, though, that none of them had bargained for. Out of the smoking mass in front of him came a blazing figure, shrieking horribly, a policeman felled but not killed in the rush, his uniform on fire. The human torch staggered, his hands reaching out in dreadful supplication to Crowther and collapsed a few feet away from the vehicle. The man jerked helplessly on the ground for several seconds, his limbs being eaten away and Crowther began to cry in shame and self-disgust. To think he had enjoyed firing the weapon!

When the thick smoke, carrying the hideous smell of roasting human flesh, began to clear, a fleet of small airplanes, two-seaters, was flying low down the road between the houses. When the planes reached the vast army of animals who had got to within fifty yards of the end of the road, they sprayed sheets of liquid from their tails, but it seemed to have no effect on the cats. Close behind came helicopters, half a dozen of them. The whirling birds descended in a group and each delivered a jet of flame towards the ground.

In an instant the cats had become a blanket of fire, the flames leaping a full twenty feet into the air, narrowly avoiding the last helicopter as it pulled out of its dive. Cats flew in all directions to avoid the blaze, but were soon consumed, their bodies on fire, smoke pouring from them.

The flames continued to spread threateningly until several of the nearby houses were smoking, but soon the reassuring clanging bells of the fire engines told them that everything was under control. The troops began to move in from the end of the road to pick off any animals that might have miraculously survived the inferno.

There was a shout near to Crowther, who still straddled the back seat of his car. Jock Campbell was shouting the order for the jeeps to advance once more and catch up with the troops ahead. Crowther looked around, saw that the Army had advanced about a hundred yards while the battles had been fought behind them, and leapt back into the driving seat, trying to dismiss the sight of the burning policeman from his mind. He consoled himself with the thought that he had only done what was necessary, and gunned the jeep into life.

The police regrouped behind the vehicles and, as they advanced, small detachments were sent to search each house to ensure that no further surprises were going to be sprung on them from hiding animals.

As the car passed by his flat, Inglis craned his neck. He leapt from the jeep without warning, landed in an untidy heap on the ground, jumped to his feet in one movement and was running towards the apartment. He had seen a soldier emerging dragging a large body behind him. As he came up to the soldier, he froze in horror. He was gazing down into the dead, mutilated eyes of his father, the senator. Minutes earlier he had been needlessly wondering what he would say to the man if they met. Now he just stood, mouth gaping soundlessly, his eyes filling with tears that began to stream down his face.

As if in a dream, he stumbled through the entrance and down the steps, almost slipping in the pool of heavy, dark-red blood just by the doorway. He walked unsteadily to his desk over the toppled cages, stepping on the bodies of dead cats. He sat down in his desk chair, and placed his head disconsolately in his hands. It was several moments before he noticed the note lying in front of him. He picked it up, opened the page and started reading. Even though it was a short letter, Inglis could tell that a lot of care had gone into it. He could hear his father talking as he read it. When he had finished, he let it fall from his fingers. It wafted slowly to the ground. To think that he had so often thought of killing his father and now to find out that, perhaps, they could have achieved some sort of understanding. And now it was too late, for he had killed him. He had been responsible for everything, and now his experiments had resulted in the death of the man who he had hated for so long without ever really knowing.

Inglis stared around the room. At the foot of the nearest wall lay a huge black cat, its jaws open, a gaping hole in its throat where the acid had eaten through. Inglis wondered whether he really had any right to live after what he had done.

Crowther had thought for an instant of stopping to follow Inglis, but had decided against it. There were more important things to be done. He listened intently to his walkie-talkie as he drove. The smaller detachments of cats on parallel streets had been easily beaten back, and, as he pulled the jeep to a halt behind the line of soldiers, the plan seemed to have worked perfectly. The eastern cordon of troops had moved to within one hundred yards of their western companions. Crowther had been worried about so many of the cats disappearing underground during the chase, but he had been assured by the Army that that was to be expected and that they had the situation firmly under control.

The cats were strangely passive under the constant cross-fire of flames and bullets. They seemed uninterested in the fact that their numbers—Crowther estimated them at roughly five thousand—were slowly being whittled away. The troops had stopped moving and were firing with pleasure into the midst of their foe. Their officers shouted orders for the lines to be kept closed and for no breaks to be allowed. The animals were waiting for something. That was obvious.

From the back seat of the car, Fred Dempsey began shouting for his son. With a start, Crowther realized that the boy was nowhere to be seen. As he screwed up his eyes to get a better view through the flames and the smoke, there was a sudden hush amongst the soldiers and all firing abruptly ceased. Rising slowly from the ground, the cats moving apart as he emerged, was Mark Dempsey. Around him stood his bodyguard of black cats.

"MARK!" His father's scream echoed strangely in the sudden silence. "MARK!" The boy, some fifty yards away, turned to look at him but there was no sign of recognition in his eyes. Dempsey tried to move again, but the professor still had his restraining arms around him. The child raised his arms above his head and turned slowly until he was facing the west. Crowther gasped in astonishment. The eyes of every one of the five thousand cats was trained upon him. That's why they had been so calm, so composed. They had been waiting for a signal. The soldiers gawped as well, unable to bring themselves to shoot at the boy and their officers had given no orders for them to resume firing.

This was it, Crowther realized, as the boy stood perfectly still, facing away from them. The final act was about to take place, and it was all up to the boy.

The child brought both arms, which had been raised above his head, down sharply, pointing straight in front of him. As if galvanized by a mighty electric shock, the cats surged forward, aiming for the point in the line towards which Mark was pointing. Crowther watched in amazement as the troops stepped back, breaking the line. Like water escaping from a bath, the cats swirled towards the gap which was quickly transformed into a thirty-yard exit. As they ran between the soldiers, they had to face a gauntlet of fire, but nothing could halt them.

At last the troops acted. The whole of the eastern line surged forward after the escaping cats. Jock Campbell signaled for the people in the jeeps to dismount and follow on foot. Crowther jumped to the ground and began to chase after the soldiers, pursued by Inglis, Vole and Dempsey. They halted after fifty yards. Both cordons of troops had now formed into one and were grouped around a large, derelict building that Crowther could not at once identify. Then it hit him. The abandoned church, right at the edge of the area. The animals were pouring in through the broken windows and the open door. So that was why they had remained undetected. The building, which was obviously the cats' lair, stood some twenty-five yards outside the protected area. Their attacks had been made from there through underground tunnels. There could be no other explanation. But why, Crowther wondered, had the Army allowed them to get inside? They would just pour out again through their underground escape routes. His question was partially answered by a loud booming sound. A section of the church roof blew straight into the air. More explosions followed. The remaining section of one of the windows burst outwards, scattering glass and animal limbs.

So the Army had planned it all along. The lair had been found and explosives planted. The dead bodies discovered in the radio station. It all came back to him. This was the plan Andrews had initiated but not expanded upon.

Somewhere behind him he could hear a woman screeching out a girl's name. How had civilians got into the area? He turned back to look at the building. The last of the cats was going through the door. The soldiers were frantically busy. They obviously had something big planned.

A little girl tottered forward from the front line of troops and with small dotting steps walked towards the gaping entrance to the building. No one moved. They were paralyzed with horror. She had crawled unseen amongst the preoccupied soldiers and was walking to her certain death.

Suddenly, a figure darted out of the crowd as the girl wobbled into the church. Crowther recognized Inglis as the young American covered the space between the soldiers and the door in a few giant strides.

Inglis, who had been walking slowly back towards the center of the action, had seen the child move towards the building and had known at once what he had to do. Once inside the church, he strained his eyes in the darkness to catch sight of her. The little girl was humming to herself. "Nice pussy," he heard her coo. She was standing some five yards from him. In one motion he launched himself forward, grabbed her around the waist, and hurled her with great force through the open door, praying that his violent action would not harm her. He had no choice. As soon as he tried to follow, however, he found himself being dragged to the ground. He struggled madly and managed to twist himself onto his back. He was staring into the eyes of Mark Dempsey. He tried to smile.

"Hallo, Mark," he choked out. Mark smiled back. It chilled Inglis. He began to struggle afresh, but something was holding him down. He moved his head to look. Each of his limbs was pinned by a huge black cat like the dead one he had found in his laboratory, their lips drawn back over their fangs. He looked at Mark, whose head was moving in closer. The boy had exactly the same expression as the cats on his face, and his discolored teeth were smeared with fresh blood. As the boy's moving head brushed against Inglis's ear, the American could hear a shocking, soft purring noise emanating from Mark's throat. With a massive effort, he hauled himself to his feet, and when he found Mark still clinging to his neck, teeth snapping loudly together in thin air, he pulled back his fist and punched the boy straight in the solar plexus. He heard him gasp and his arms slithered apart. Inglis spun around and made for the door. He caught sight of the waiting soldiers before crashing back onto the ground. He tried to move his head but it was being held firmly in place by what felt like human fingers. He could feel the hot breath of the boy as his teeth grazed against his exposed neck. Then there was a searing pain as his flesh was torn away in one great mouthful. He made one last attempt to move and managed to crawl the two feet to the open door. A shot rang out. The hold on his back loosened. He twisted over to see the naked boy receding into the darkness, blood pouring from a bullet wound in his shoulder. Within seconds, he could feel strong arms dragging him across the stone pathway leading from the building. They laid him gently on the pavement where his lifeblood oozed out onto the street. He opened his eyes, Crowther was hunched over him, staring down anxiously. He shifted his head slightly. Vole was looking at him as well. "It's justice," he whispered. His neck muscles went limp and he was dead.

Crowther had barely had time to stand upright when Fred Dempsey bumped into him.

"And where the hell are you going?" he asked.

"That's my son in there," the MP shouted. "They want to burn down the building. I've got to save him." Crowther motioned for two soldiers to hold the distraught man.

"He's no more your son than he is mine. That thing in there just killed this man by ripping a chunk out of his neck. Do you really think that your son could do that?"

Crowther turned to face the Army colonel who had been in the conference room with them.

"Sorry," the colonel said, "you'll have to move back. We're going to burn the whole damn place down. Everything's ready. We've got men posted at the various exit tunnels we found during the night, just in case any of them survive. I doubt it," he added with obvious relish.

Crowther and Vole moved back. Some fifty flamethrowers were trained on the building. The colonel raised his arm, held it aloft for several seconds and let it fall. As if expelling one giant breath from hell, the machines opened up and a massive white-hot flame licked the whole façade of the church. The muted roar lasted for thirty seconds. When it had stopped, the building had lit up like a paper castle. Behind the crackle of burning timber and the clatter of falling stone they could hear the obscene, high-pitched shrieking of the dying animals trapped in the inescapable inferno. A hail of grenades followed and the whole building shook with the violence of the explosions. Cats, their bodies singed and burning, began pouring from the windows and the main door to be met by rapid, deadly volleys of machine-gun fire.

Crowther stood and gaped at the scene and, as he watched, began to sob with relief. They had been so close to total destruction.

There was a shout from the soldiers. Some were pointing up towards the sky. Crowther followed their pointing hands and saw, high above them, a solitary figure crouched on the one small sliver of the church's roof that remained intact.

Mark Dempsey, crouched over the furthest point of the roof, his face a horrifying mask of naked hatred, his body charred by the flames, blood pouring from the wound in his shoulder, glowered down at the expectant crowd, hissing and snarling in fury and agony.

"Kill him," Crowther shouted, unable to watch any longer. "For God's sake, shoot him down."

The colonel motioned to one of his marksmen. The soldier knelt down, hoisted the rifle to his shoulder and took careful aim. Just as his finger began to squeeze on the trigger, a shape lunged at him. Fred Dempsey's despairing gesture came too late. The gun fired, the bullet catching the child full in the chest.

The boy looked down at the crimson explosion on his body, blinked several times as if coming to his senses, and then plummeted forward off the building with a terrifying scream that stopped the instant his body thudded on the ground below.

The lady nestled thankfully into the corner of the bench. It was nice to be able to take the dog for a walk in the park again. She didn't see why it had taken them so long to open it up to the public. After all, the cats had all been destroyed nearly two weeks previously. All that time to get those poor evacuees back into their homes. It didn't seem fair, and then having every animal in London in to check for disease. Just like the authorities to overreact, she thought.

"Rupert," she called softly, but the Black Labrador was nowhere to be seen. She didn't mind. After all, it was a treat for him to get back on the grass again.

When she felt the gentle pressure on her leg she let her arm fall by her side, expecting the reassuring caress of Rupert's warm muzzle, but there was nothing there. She leant over the side of the bench. The kitten gazed up at her appealingly. "Oh, you sweet thing," she murmured and gently extended her hand. The tiny animal, fawn-colored and about nine inches long, kept its startled eyes on the object as it moved towards him. It waited until the hand was no more than an inch away, opened its mouth and sank its small, sharp teeth firmly into the welcoming flesh. The woman screamed and began to shake her arm. The kitten disengaged itself just as the large dog came bounding out of the undergrowth. The Labrador chased after the scurrying cat until it came to some trees. The tiny animal skated up the side of the bark and edged along the low overhanging branch until it could see the annoyed dog standing directly below, baying at the sky in frustration.

The kitten and the dog locked eyes. The dog stopped barking. After thirty seconds it began to edge slowly backwards. There was something in the kitten's expression it didn't like.

ABOUT THE AUTHOR

NICK SHARMAN is the author of eight horror novels, which have sold over a million copies in total. His fiction has been published by New English Library, New American Library, Hamlyn, Corgi and McLelland & Stewart, and his books have been translated into a number of languages, including Spanish, Italian and Japanese. Nick began writing when he was NEL's publicity manager in the late 1970s. He started with tales of historical adventure, but the emergence of Stephen King and James Herbert—and the fact that he was a lifelong horror fan—convinced him to switch genres. The success of his first horror novel, *The Cats*, allowed him to write full-time. Seven years later—with six more books published in the US and the UK, including the bestselling The Surrogate—he joined the BBC as a producer on its main TV news bulletin. A stint editing live political programmes at Westminster followed. For some reason, the BBC made him homepage editor of its new website, then head of interactive TV, where his team kept winning awards. Retired now, he lives in London with his wife and son. He blogs most days. Keep it to yourself, but his real name is Scott Grønmark. He's still afraid of the dark—and he has no idea who wrote all those scary books.

Curious about other Crossroad Press books?
Stop by our site:
http://store.crossroadpress.com
We offer quality writing
in digital, audio, and print formats.

Printed in Great Britain
by Amazon

63023311R00087